WINNING THE ORC'S HEART

TROLLKIN LOVERS BOOK SEVEN

LYONNE RILEY

Introduction

Graz is an inventor, utterly obsessed with magic and its hidden history. While following clues toward the source, he meets a human woman investigating the very same ancient ruin—unleashing a rivalry between them to get to the next clue first.

As a member of the King's History Corps, it's Vienne's job to reveal what she learns to her boss, but now that she's seen the power of magic for herself, she wonders whether it's safe to spill its secrets before she can uncover the truth.

Soon, Graz and Vienne both begin to experience a magical sickness. But when a taboo spark erupts between them, magic will either save them—or doom them.

Content Warnings

May contain spoilers.

- Graphic depictions of sex
- Gun violence
- Injury

- Magical violence
- Kidnapping (of FMC)
- Organized crime
- Breeding
- Surprise pregnancy

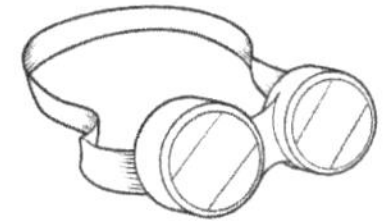

CHAPTER 1

GRAZ

The one thing I'm absolutely certain about is that magic is real. I've seen it with my own eyes. I've experimented on it. I've witnessed what it can do, and it's just as marvelous and powerful as it is dangerous.

I slow my horse, Jaks, and glance down at my map. I'm approaching the third-closest marker, and I should be there within the day, as long as whatever used to be out here still exists. So far, though, I've had miserable luck.

The first ruin—which was closest to home—collapsed, utterly destroying any evidence of what was inside it. I still can't believe my idiot best friend, Lo'zar, obliterated an ancient site to save his and his woman's hide.

I never pictured that horny player would settle down. He'd always been the first to find a pretty face in a bar and head upstairs. He lived a life in the shadows, flitting from one bed to the next, one job to another.

Yet... something in him changed when he found her. Lo'zar

told me that he'd come across his mate, the one destined for him, the very thing that few of us trollkin ever manage to come across in our lifetimes.

And he'd discovered it in a human.

I can't deny that it makes me wild with envy. That asshole. Yeah, sure, I'm happy for him, but it's so unfair. Finding a true mate of my own is unlikely at best, and seeing my playboy friend get what I've always wanted bites.

Gritting my teeth, I steer my horse off to the right and follow the fork in the road, veering deeper into the swampland. It's slow going, even with what remains of a path here. My horse's hooves sink deep in the mud, and he grumbles under me as he lifts his foot out and continues plodding along.

The pyramid that Lo'zar destroyed wasn't the only evidence of magic to go down in flames. So did my second lead. Quite literally, it exploded.

That experience does unsettle me.

When I'd gotten to the second mark on the map, outside the neutral city of Morgenzan, I'd found a great battle under-way. The city guard and a pack of wild orcs had picked a fight with one another, and in the middle of the scuffle, the top of the mountain blew right off.

Most certainly the work of magic.

I had waited in the city for the fires to cool, and then I'd gone in the middle of the night to inspect the remains, only to find the mine had collapsed, and all evidence of any magic that might have been there was gone, too.

I grumbled the entire train ride home. Waste of a trip—and a long one, as far north as it was.

Now I'm headed to the third marker on the map I pilfered out of one of the boss's shipments. All his illicit goods come through my mechanic shop, and Kugara doesn't mind giving me a first look at the "intellectual" things, as she calls them:

books, maps, and rolls of parchment paper with ancient inscriptions. Gusak smuggles historical relics like this for collectors and other individuals of disrepute, and he wasn't going to notice one scrap of paper missing. Kugara had kindly looked the other way when I took the map, and Gusak hadn't been any the wiser.

That's for the best, because our boss doesn't take too kindly to disobedience or petty larceny. But the moment I saw that map, I knew it was special, and it was worth the risk.

I've since redrawn it, leaving the original curled up on a shelf in my shop where it won't get damaged. I have two replicas with me, the other wrapped up in my saddlebag in case I drop the first one in the mud.

Considering that it's me, a very likely thing to happen.

I hope that when I find whatever the map says is out here in the swamp, it won't also disappear before I can study it. All I want is another few drops of that glowing purple magic so I can finally test its limits, find out what it does, and perhaps even learn why it's here.

I curl one hand around the vial at my neck. It's the last few drops of magic I have after building the amulet for Lo'zar and his human. I'd had to do so many experiments to get it right that at the end, I was left with only this.

Deciding to leave it raw, just in case I need it later, I poured it all into a reinforced vial so it couldn't escape into the world by accident. I hope that I never have to use it, because I still don't truly know what it's capable of—though the explosion up north gave me some hint as to the breadth of magic's destructive power.

I may not know much, but there are legends of humans and trollkin alike who once wielded such things, and I'm beginning to wonder if those legends aren't founded in reality, at least in part.

Wouldn't it be amazing if they were? If all the stories we grew up on were true? That would be the discovery of the century. I could use it to power all sorts of devices. Who knows what I could create?

The sun crosses the sky as Jaks and I wade deeper into the swamp, and the mud grows ever thicker. We pass dead trees, cattails, and ponds with lurking creatures in them. Around midday I come across some dry land, where I dig out my rations and chew the dried meat while Jaks browses for what grass he can find.

For an orc who hates travel, I sure chose a peculiar path. I miss fresh-cooked meals with a mug of bubbling beer. I can't hunt to save my life, so dried rations is what I get. Believe me, I tried a few times to bring down prey, and it was an embarrassment for me as much as it was for the rabbit. Even Jaks judged me.

But I know I'm close to my destination now. I can almost taste it. And when I get there, maybe I'll finally have answers to all my questions.

The trees grow denser as we reach the point where I have to venture off the beaten path. My horse does not like this idea, and objects vehemently as I guide him away from the road and into the deeper mud. His hooves stick with every step, and soon he comes to an abrupt halt.

He won't go any farther.

Fuck. I need my damned horse, and I can't leave him here tied up to a tree, either. What if I don't come back?

That's a haunting thought, but one I must seriously consider after seeing what's become of the other two markers. If there's magic here, who knows what could happen?

I hop off Jaks's back and try leading him instead. He goes a bit farther now that I'm not weighing him down, but the path becomes more treacherous the more distance there is between us and the main road. I just have to hope I estimated my destination right.

Finally, one of my legs sinks into the mud up to the knee. Damn it, that's not good. Jaks stops again, unwilling to risk life and limb for me in the swamp, and I don't really blame him.

I'm about to turn back around when I peer up at the sky, and there, I see it: a rock face, high above the branches. Something that definitely does not belong in the middle of a swamp.

"Fine," I tell my horse, wrapping his reins around a tree. "Wait here. I'm going to take a look."

He huffs and takes a bite of a reed instead.

Squaring my shoulders and sliding my goggles down over my eyes, I head off toward the structure, even as the mud threatens to swallow me up. I'm going to find answers, no matter what it takes.

I need to know the truth. I need to understand why magic exists, why it found me, and what I'm meant to do with it.

VIENNE

Raiden is such a fucking asshole.

"Gear up, everyone," he says, his rifle slung over his shoulder. "We're almost at the target location. We have no idea what we'll find there."

He likes acting as if the King's History Corps is some kind of military unit, when we're really all just a bunch of intellectuals. We like relics and artifacts, investigation and understanding.

He pauses in front of me. Everyone knows that Raiden and I have a sexual relationship. We tried to keep it under wraps for a time, but it was too obvious when we disappeared into the same tent together and the others could hear us gasping. Instead of treating his "girlfriend" with favoritism, though, he's even harder on me than the other members of the Corps, as if to show them he has no bias toward me.

"You're heading in first, Vienne," he says, pointing a finger in my face. "Go down, take a look around, and come back with your report. I want to know what to expect down there."

Just great. I don't even get a partner? Of course Raiden would never go down himself, not when he has a minion to take the brunt of whatever we might discover.

I'm never sneaking into his tent with him again.

I get to my feet, working hard not to show how he pisses me off, and straighten my clothes. I run a hand across my gun on one hip and my pick axe on the other, then check my pack to make sure I have my tools. I might find what we're after buried under dirt or sand or even rock, and then I'll have to chip away at it to get to what I want.

"Sure thing, *boss*," I tell him.

Raiden smirks. "Good."

We all get prepped, and then it's time. The ruin rises high overhead, a rather monstrous figure in the otherwise misty, dead swamp. Yesterday we studied the exterior, investigating how carefully the massive stones were laid at a time so far in the past. How did they manage to move these? Now we have trains, which can carry great objects a long way, but back then? Each rock making up the ancient building is set in such a way that it doesn't even need mortar to hold it together. Instead, the pieces are fitted with notches, creating tall walls that still haven't given way to time.

Upon further investigation, we'd found an entrance covered by piles of vines we had to carefully cut and burn away. Then we spent two days trying to discover just how that entrance *opened*. It was clearly a door, but made of stone and far too heavy for us to move, even with the entire Corps working on it together.

Yesterday, though, just when we thought we might need to give up and bring in the military to help us chip our way through it, one of the other jerk-offs on the team found a button. When he pressed his hand to the circle of stone, it gave way, sinking into the wall.

And then the door opened. We didn't dare close it again, so we left it that way, exposed to the elements.

Today it's my turn to descend into the darkness with nothing but a fire starter and a torch to light my way. When we reach the top of the steps that lead to the entrance, the rest of the Corps members gather around.

"Don't fuck this up," Raiden says, and I scowl. I don't know what I was thinking by sleeping with him in the first place. Maybe he's a bit less abrasive when we're alone together, but no dick is worth this.

"Yeah, yeah." I wave him off as I light my torch, then start down the steps. The way is narrow and the stairs are steep, but I've seen much worse. Nothing compares to the time I had to climb a rope out of a dank pit filled with rotting corpses because we had a lead on some ancient burial ground. It was there, of course, underneath the disgusting offal both modern and ancient, so we had to remove the corpses in order to dig.

That's my job, though, and most of the time I enjoy it. Being a part of the King's History Corps is an honor not granted to many. I had to demonstrate a knowledge of ancient languages, world geography, and history to be eligible. My role here is important enough to keep me out of military conflicts, but we're still paid well.

Best of all, we get to learn the secrets of the past and uncover mysteries that no one else has ever pieced together. Usually all we find is some ancient statue with big tits, but occasionally we come across a clue that tells us more about our origins, and that's when it's all worthwhile. We've found burial sites with evidence of how humans once laid our dead to rest, and artwork carved into stone caverns that tells us about how our ancestors lived. Ancient humans were hunter-gatherers, struggling every day to survive against predators and the elements—and often against trollkin, too.

I descend deeper and deeper into the ruin, and the walls hug me closer. But claustrophobia is not one of my faults, or else I'd never be doing this work in the first place. Spiders cover the rock faces, though they recede into the stonework as I pass with my torch. Spiders, snakes, and scorpions don't love fire, to my benefit.

I'm wondering just how far down this goes, imagining I've already descended beneath the ground, when the torchlight catches something up ahead.

While the tunnel appears to end, the stairs continue on into what appears to be a large room. Yes! I could pump a fist into the air. This must be what we're looking for. The joy of discovery washes over me—the reason I do this job in the first place.

When I take a step down into the cavernous space, I gasp. It's fucking *huge*. The massive stone room spreads out around me. Hundreds of people could have gathered here once upon a time without much difficulty, and I'm guessing they did by the stone thrones erected on the far end of the massive room and the floors rubbed shiny by many feet.

But there's very little else here besides the thrones. Intricate carvings decorate the walls, though, and as I descend the steps toward the floor, I raise my torch to get a good look at them.

"What the hell?" I come to a stop as I take in the image etched into the wall. There are two figures facing one another:

one human, eyes wide open. The other is certainly trollkin, with tusks rising from the sides of its mouth. I may not have seen any up close before, but everyone knows what they look like. We have paintings and history books depicting the centuries of war between us.

I stare at the wall, trying to make sense of what I'm seeing. What are these images doing here? What is this room trying to tell me?

Now this is a discovery. I'm sure the King would be fascinated by it.

That's when I hear a noise. It's faint footsteps, coming from down below. I pause on the stairs as I search the room for the source, and find a doorway on the other end of the room, behind the two thrones. A light bobs up and down along the wall.

My mouth falls open when someone appears there. He is large and green, with massive shoulders, and what are clearly two white tusks protruding from his mouth. His hair is wild around his head, barely tamed by a pair of goggles.

A fucking trollkin.

Chapter 2

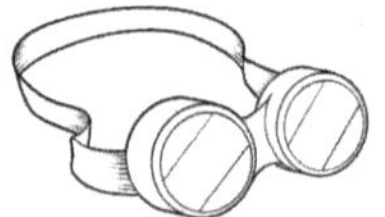

Graz

I got lucky—extremely lucky. After investigating the south side of the massive stone structure, I discovered an old, hidden doorway covered by fallen rocks and vines. Luckily, I was able to move most of them aside. There are benefits to being an orc, and one of them is my upper body strength.

After discovering this perfect little side entrance, I went back to retrieve my horse and settled in for the night somewhere dry, nearly bouncing with my excitement to return the next morning and investigate. I barely got any sleep, but that doesn't matter much when the thrill of finding answers is coursing through my blood.

What if there's more magic here, like the map suggests? I can do so much with it, learn so much *from* it. Maybe I could make other devices like the one I created for Lo'zar. What else could I build with that kind of power in my hands?

I light my lamp first thing in the morning and head back. I designed it so I wouldn't have to carry a torch, because holding a stick of fire near my head doesn't entice me. It safely contains the flames, and I built in special reflectors to amplify the light.

The passageway is pitch black inside, but my lamp guides the way, revealing cobwebs in every corner and tiny creatures fleeing wherever the firelight touches them. I even spot a snake that slithers off into a hole in the stone the moment I go past.

I shudder. I very much do not like snakes. Lizards? Fine. Izzy is still back at my mechanic's shop, and I hope Kugara is feeding him. I thought about bringing my iguana along, but managing a finicky horse and a territorial lizard at the same time felt like too much work.

Snakes, on the other hand... The last thing I need is a venomous bite while I'm out in the middle of nowhere all alone.

The passageway winds deeper into the stone fortress, and I wonder just where it's taking me. Carvings cover the walls, figures and shapes that must be some form of language. I observe them as I walk, thinking I'll have to return later to make rubbings. Perhaps I can decode it if I find some context deeper inside.

I'm starting to breathe harder the farther I get in the tunnel, imagining all of these rocks tumbling down on top of me. I would be trapped, probably crushed.

Just as I'm about to turn around, because the walls feel like they're growing narrower and narrower... I find it. The hallway ends, and my lamp illuminates something else just beyond it. With a few more steps, I find myself standing out in the open, in a massive room that spreads out around me in every direction.

This is what I've been searching for. I've made it. Plus, I survived that tiny tunnel.

That's when I hear a sharp cry. On the other end of the huge space, someone is standing high up on the steps, a torch in her hand. Another person? Here, in a ruin that hasn't been touched in thousands of years?

Her outfit is brownish beige, a matching buttoned shirt and matching pants. She's staring at me just as I'm staring at her.

A fucking *human.*

That's when I notice the gun. Damn it. I didn't even think to bring a weapon with me. I never, ever expected I'd find someone else here—not to mention a human.

Instantly her fingers grasp handle of her gun, and I know I'm screwed. Absolutely fucked.

I hold up both my hands, the lamp dangling from one of them. If I show her I'm not armed, maybe she won't shoot. Humans and trollkin have established a tentative peace in the last few years, after the last war wreaked havoc on both our peoples. I have to hope that truce extends to the two of us, as well.

She pulls the gun from her hip and takes a few more steps down the stairs, but it doesn't look like she's ready to shoot just yet. Now we're standing across from one another, separated by a few hundred yards. The two stone thrones stand between us, and I suppose I could hide behind one of them if she started shooting.

I can't believe I didn't come prepared. I'm such an idiot.

"*Saan haas!*" the human calls out, her shoulders tense. I wish I knew what the hell she was saying. At least Lo'zar and his human mate had some kind of mind-speak, where they could communicate without words, allowing them to cross the language barrier.

Unfortunately, I have no such abilities.

"Hey," I call back, waving my hands in the air. "Please don't kill me. I'm not armed, see?" I gesture to my belt, where I only carry my excavation tools.

The human's brows lower. Then, to my surprise, she returns the gun to her holster. She holds up her torch and cocks her head like she's trying to figure me out.

"I'm just here to investigate," I try again. "I'm safe. I won't hurt you if you don't hurt me."

The human frowns, probably because she can't understand me just as much as I can't understand her. We're at an impasse.

With a sigh, the human turns away from me. It's such a foolish move that I'm tempted to run across the room and hit her over the head just to eliminate the threat of her pulling a gun on me. But I came here to find answers, not fight with humans. So I watch what she's going to do, keeping a safe distance between us.

The little woman approaches the wall, holding up her torch. An image is etched into the rock from floor to ceiling, and she's staring at it intently, like she's trying to figure it out.

When I take a few steps back to see the whole thing, I immediately understand why. The picture is clear: two faces, pointed toward each other—one human, the other trollkin. In the middle, near the floor, there are two hands locked together.

"What the fuck?" I say reflexively. The human's head jerks toward me, and she shakes her head, putting a finger to her lips to shush me.

Huh. At least some gestures are universal.

I decide to obey the woman who has a gun at her hip, even though it annoys me to be shut up like a child. At least I've interacted with humans before, and I know they're not all little wretches. Rimi, Lo'zar's mate, had irritated me at first, but after a while, she grew on me. All she wanted was to be with my best friend and find her way to safety. How could I hate her when that's what we all want?

This human, though... I have no such assurances that she won't try to kill me.

But I'm too curious for caution to reign. Deciding to push my luck, I carry my own lantern closer to the carvings on the wall. What does this mean? Did these ruins belong to trollkin, or to humans, once upon a time? I examine the other walls, holding up my lamp higher. The exact same carving is repeated behind us, as well, the faces so close together they look like they're about to kiss.

The human appears just as perplexed by it. What have we found down here?

Vienne

The orc's got a peculiar device—a lit flame contained with in a protective glass case and equipped with a handle. I didn't think trollkin were all that advanced, but I'm starting to see I might've been wrong.

What's the chance that we would both arrive here at the same time, in this ancient ruin deep in the swamp? It's unfathomable that we'd happen to discover it at the same moment, and yet, here we are.

What's he after?

He doesn't seem keen to attack, given he has no weapons, and I don't want to start a fight if I don't have to. I could always call Raiden and the team, and they'd have him surrounded and outnumbered in seconds—but for some reason, I don't think that's necessary. He's not interested in me, that's clear. No, he's curious about what we've discovered, too. Could I have found a fellow scholar?

Part of me wishes I could speak their language. I want to

know why he's here, if he's after the same secrets I am. The King's History Corps has been cataloguing ancient ruins for quite a few years now, looking for remnants of our past, and occasionally stumbling across some hidden treasure.

Maybe he's a grave robber, but I don't think he'll find that here. This ruin isn't a grave or a tomb. I think it's a gathering place, perhaps the seat of some ancient king or queen, if the matching thrones are any indication.

While the orc quietly puzzles over the carvings on the wall, I investigate further, searching the corners. There are bugs galore living here, and I have to push away cobwebs to get a good look at the rock faces. More carvings decorate the rest of the room, these ones appearing to be more like a pictographic script. A script that looks familiar.

I hastily pull out some paper, place it against the wall, and rub my charcoal over it to capture the etchings. I use more and more sheets, trying to record the entire length of it, rolling them up and putting them in my bag when I've finished.

I've seen some of these characters before in one other ruin we found in the desert of the Hazrain. That was quite an expedition, and one I would rather not repeat. The sand there is brutal. All we found was the tippy-top of a ruin that had mostly sunk into the sand, but after a few days of laborious excavating, we managed to dig out some stones with carvings on them—carvings that looked like these.

Is it really possible they're connected when they're so far apart? Could the same people, whether human or trollkin, have actually built cities in both places?

"*Grrak haz arg,*" someone says behind me, and I spin around with my charcoal held out like a knife. I'm not sure what I plan on doing with it, but maybe I could jab it into the orc's eye.

He tilts his head at me, standing a few feet away, and

glances down at the outstretched charcoal in my hand. Then he grabs hold of the big, thick goggles on his head, pulls them down over his eyes, and walks up beside me. I put a few feet of distance between us, but he ignores me, crouching down to get a better look at the carvings. There, he taps a button on top of his goggles.

A tiny metal arm emerges, and I jump back in surprise as it lets out a tinny, mechanical whine. The arm has what appears to be a single lens attached to it, and it settles in front of his goggles. He closes his other eye, peering through the magnifying lens.

"*Urzag grrozek,*" he says, though I think he's talking to himself, not to me. He hums, then sits back on his heels and taps the button again. The tiny lens retracts into his goggles again, and he pulls them back up onto his head.

This moment should be significantly less companionable than it is. He's trollkin. I'm human. We're underground in a massive, ancient ruin together, simply observing and recording.

"*Naz?*" the orc asks me, nodding at the sheaf of paper in my hand. Reluctantly, I hold it out, and he takes it with incredible gentleness. He unrolls the paper and cocks his head, then hands it back to me.

I'm not sure what that was about.

Then the orc rises up to his feet and leaves me again, wandering over to the other side of the room to keep searching. I decide to ignore him for now and continue with my work—as strange as this all is.

But after only a few moments, he calls out to me: "*Yazzen!*"

I turn around and find him beckoning me over. My hand drops to the handle of my gun reflexively, and the orc frowns. He shakes his head like he's disappointed in me, and returns to observing the big mural carved onto the other wall.

"Fine," I grumble, then head toward him. The orc is tracing the carving around the room with his index finger, and when I approach, he ushers me to follow him back to the center, where the two hands are clasped.

"*Azz yak*," he says, pointing at something. I stoop to get a closer look, where two circles appear to be cut into the stone. Pressed into them are a pair of handprints: one with five fingers, and a larger one with four fingers.

I glance at the orc, and he's tapping his chin thoughtfully. Then he lowers his four-fingered hand to the matching print and sets his palm against it, fitting his fingers into the grooves. Reflexively, I do the same thing, fitting my hand neatly into the five-fingered print etched into the stone.

Both circles abruptly depress, sinking into the wall. I gasp and yank my hand away, afraid it might get sucked into some sort of booby trap and cut off. The orc stumbles back, just as surprised.

Then, all around us, there comes a deep and terrible groaning, as if the rocks themselves are moving.

What have we just done?

CHAPTER 3

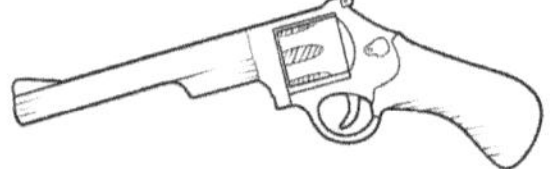

The orc jumps to his feet, securing his goggles over his eyes as he tries to locate the source of the sound. The terrible rumbling continues, and I stumble when the floor itself shakes.

"Fuck!" Instinctually I grab onto the closest object to hold myself up—which is, unfortunately, my companion's big arm. His eyes are wide as he also reaches out for support, landing against the wall and trying not to fall over as the stones underneath us shift and groan.

Then, suddenly, it stops. The floor goes still again, and silence falls around us. I realize I'm still clutching him, and quickly let go, putting space between us.

"Uh, sorry," I say, rubbing my hand. But something else has caught his attention.

"*Zag!*" The orc points at something over my shoulder. "*Ag yak zag!*"

I don't know what this means, but I understand the

gesture. I spin around to find that in the middle of the room, the floor has separated, leaving a huge hole. From it, something is now rising up—something irregular in shape, almost egg-like. We both take a few steps back so we're up against the wall, and stare as the big object emerges. It appears to be on a pedestal, and as it approaches the surface, it slows down.

Then, when the pedestal is flat with the floor, it stops and lets out a soft *click!*

Neither of us moves.

"What the hell?" I take a step toward the rock, but a big, green arm shoots out, blocking my path. I glare at the orc, but he shakes his head, and the fear is written plain on his face. We just triggered some ancient mechanism, and we have no way of knowing what we did—or what this huge rock-looking object is.

"Fine," I say, pushing him away and crossing my arms. "What do you suggest?"

He rolls his eyes, clearly unable to understand me, either. He gets down on his knees and pulls off his pack, then rifles around inside. After a moment, he withdraws something small tucked in his hand.

"What is that?" I ask as he rises to his feet again. Extending his arm, he opens his fingers to reveal what looks like a very large bug.

I put up my hands to protect myself, and the orc guffaws. He dangles it by one leg, holding it out to me. It's not moving, so it must not be alive. My curiosity demands I lean closer and get a better look.

Wait. That's no bug. It has tiny metal legs, each joint attached by a very small gear. Grinning, the orc crouches down and drops the bug on the floor, then pokes it in the back.

Then the tiny thing *gets up*. With a whirring noise, it proceeds to move forward, each of its legs tapping the ground as it goes. Slowly it approaches the big rock in the middle of the room, on a straight collision course.

I've never seen anything like it in my life. Did he make this? He has a smug expression, so I think so.

When the bug runs into the rock, it can't move forward any longer despite its scrabbling legs. With a quick nod, the orc stands up again and proceeds to walk towards it.

"Hey!" I call out, but he ignores me as he strides confidently across the room. I jog after him. "You don't know if it's safe!"

He glances at me over his shoulder and smirks. When he reaches the rock, he kneels down and picks up his bug, pressing the top to turn it off again. Then he pops it back in his bag.

I stay a safe distance away as he runs a hand over the surface. I've only come across a few booby traps in my years with the King's History Corps, but an axe almost taking off your head trains you pretty quickly to keep your distance.

The orc, however, is very much not afraid. No, he's curious as he investigates all the holes riddling the stone.

"*Yazak ag,*" he mutters to himself, rubbing his chin as he checks every side. It's almost like he's looking for something.

That's when it all starts to *glow*.

Purple light streams out from underneath the rock, and I jump as far back as I can before running into the wall. It looks almost like water, except it's twining upward, crawling through all the nooks and crannies.

The orc lets out an immense exclamation I can't understand. He reaches into one of the valleys filled with the purple substance, and I rush toward him to stop him. It could be anything. It could be dangerous.

"What are you doing?" I snap, grabbing his hand. "You could kill us both!"

The orc stares at me, then down at where I'm touching him. Suddenly, he starts laughing. He pushes me aside and then reaches in again—which is when I realize it's not water in the channels and holes.

They're *worms*.

The big, stupid orc picks one up and dangles it out in front of him, and if I had to describe his face, the word would be "gleeful."

"What is that?" I breathe, staring unabashedly as he whips out a leather pouch and drops the worm into it.

He sighs at me and shakes his head. Grabbing another one, he puts it in his palm and holds it out to me. Then he gestures at it.

"*Ag yak azan,*" he insists. I have no idea what he's saying, though.

With a roll of his eyes, the orc grabs my arm, yanks me toward him, and slaps my hand down over his.

Now stop being such a pain, comes a voice.

GRAZ

Hopefully she'll get the picture now that we've both touched the wriggly little magic creature. I made sure her hand touched it, and then I thought, *Let me talk to her.*

I'm not going to swallow the worm, though, like that idiot Lo'zar did. That's how he made the ability to communicate with his human mate permanent. As if I'd ever do something so risky—and disgusting.

Not that I need to talk to this particular human for more than a few minutes. I've gotten what I came for.

The human woman lets out a gasp when I speak in her

mind, and she stumbles backward, clutching her hand as if I've burned her. I shrug and return to the big rock, intending to collect as many of these critters as possible. Each one holds enough magic for a significant amount of experimentation. I'll be absolutely rich in the stuff after this.

"*Ayan haas?*" the human says, rubbing her head.

I don't know what you're saying, I think in her direction.

She makes some more exclamations in her language, and it's clear she's too stupid to figure it out. Ignoring her, I grab some more worms and tuck them into my bag, until it's full with the wriggling bastards. Then I tie it tightly closed and shove it in my pack.

All right. I've gotten what I need. I salute the human. *Couldn't have done it without you.*

Where the fuck is that coming from? She looks all around the room, as if it will provide some kind of clue. *What's that voice?*

Really? My eyes are about to roll out of my head.

It's me, you dolt, I say, waving my hands back and forth in front of her. *Use your mind, if you have one.*

Her mouth falls open, and her blue eyes are as big as saucers. I don't know if I'll ever get over how strange humans look, with their bright white sclera and multicolored irises.

No way. She shakes her head, as if that will clear me out of her thoughts. *This can't be happening. I'm imagining this.*

I have to laugh. *I promise, you're not.*

How the hell are you talking to me? she asks, furrowing her brow.

I don't think twice before I answer. *Magic is powerful stuff.*

Oops. I probably should have kept that to myself. It's all just too... exciting. I want to get back to my shop already and get started on experimenting.

Magic?! The human's eyes dart over to the rock that's covered in worms. *Those things?*

I don't answer. I shouldn't be telling a human about this—and certainly not demonstrating how powerful it is. It would be awful if magic fell into the hands of the human King. Who knows what kind of damage he could do with it?

How did it get here? she asks in her rather brusque voice. *How do you know all this?* Experimentally, she picks up one of the worms, holding it out in front of her as it wriggles. *Is it alive?!*

I laugh again. *I don't think so. It's what's inside them that's important.* I sling my pack onto my back, then narrow my eyes at her. *Don't tell anyone about this.*

She blinks. *Why not? This is incredible. This is a huge discovery. I can talk to you, for starters. Human and trollkin, communicating freely? That could change the entire world.*

Just great. That is my worst case scenario.

Sure, it could. Probably for the worse. I step toward her, jabbing a finger in her face. *But imagine what would happen if someone in power got hold of this. What terrible things they could accomplish.*

She tilts her head. *What's so bad about it?*

I guess I need to show her if I'm going to drill into her idiot brain how dangerous this stuff can be, how important it is that she not spread the word about what she found here today. Grabbing the worm out of her hand, I squish it in my palm and close my eyes.

Bring Izzy here, I think. Abruptly, the worm falls still.

And then the woman screeches in her language, "*Ya arya sa!*"

When I open my eyes, I find that my wish has worked, and my enormous lizard now sits on the floor between us. The woman is furious, though, and raises her foot into the air to stomp him.

Hey! Stop! I snatch Izzy up off the floor, and he flails his little legs. *Don't step on my iguana!*

That's yours? She scratches her cropped yellow hair. *Where did it come from? It wasn't here a moment ago.*

Of course not, I say, opening my other hand to drop the worm's shriveled corpse to the ground. Her eyes follow it, and her brows furrow even further. *He's here because I wished him here. He was just back home in his cage.*

I hold up Izzy in front of me, scratching his head like he enjoys. Finally, he relaxes, and I gently set him on my shoulder where he's used to perching.

You wished it here? The woman gapes at Izzy. *That doesn't make any sense.*

I'm done trying to educate her. *That's what magic does*, I say impatiently. *It will do whatever you ask of it... for the most part. The real question is, why is it here?*

That is a good question, the human admits. Her eyes travel back to the wall behind me and she squints at it. *It has something to do with that carving, I'm sure.*

I follow her gaze to the huge image of the human face and the trollkin face, with our depressed handprints at the bottom.

She might just be right about that.

But how? I walk to the carving, running one finger over the grooves. *What does it mean?*

Well, it took both of us to trigger this, whatever it is. She gestures at the big rock that emerged from the floor. *And that's what this carving implies, too. That it takes one human and one trollkin.*

She has a point there.

That's when I hear voices. They're echoing down from the hallway where I saw the human first emerge.

Who's that? I ask, narrowing my eyes. *Are you here with others?*

Her brow creases. *Yes, but they shouldn't be coming down yet.* Then it clicks in her mind—we're enemies. Our people may not be at war at this moment in time, but if there are other humans coming, that bodes very poorly for me.

Fuck! I throw on my pack and whirl toward the side entrance, where I came in. But before I can take off, a small hand wraps around my arm.

Wait! The blue-eyed woman has fear written across her face. It makes me want to protect her from whatever is coming. *If what you're saying is true, it will be bad if Raiden finds this stuff. This "magic."*

Raiden? I ask.

My boss. Do you think we can put it away? The tone of her voice is rising. *If we touch the handprints again, will it go back?*

At least something I said got through her thick skull. She doesn't want her compatriots to discover what we've found, either. And if *she* doesn't trust them, then I certainly don't.

We both crouch down at the wall and put our hands on the matching prints once more. To my surprise, the two circular depressions respond instantly, and with a creak, they both pop back out to be flush with the wall. There's another groaning sound, and the entire ruin shakes once more under our feet.

The woman stumbles, bumping into me. I grab her arm to steady her, putting my other hand on the wall. She's so small —small, and surprisingly soft to the touch. I keep her from toppling over as the huge rock in the center of the room descends once more, and the worms crawling over it speed up their movement. Suddenly, the woman darts forward and snatches one off the surface before it can fully disappear into the floor.

When it's gone, a stone circle emerges through some ancient, mechanical means I can't begin to comprehend, and covers the hole.

Then we're alone again, and the shaking ceases. Louder shouts come from the hallway, and I know it's time to go.

Sorry to cut this short, I say, releasing her. *But I have to leave.*

She gestures at my pack. *What are you going to do with those?*

I shrug. *Figure out what this stuff does. Why it's here.* I glance up at the huge carvings on the wall. *Maybe find out what this means.*

I want to know, too, she says, her lips forming a hard, determined line. *There's another ruin, in the Stoneteeth Mountains. We're going there next.*

I stare at her. Does she have the same map I have?

Guess I had better get there first, I say, heading toward the exit. For a brief moment, though, I don't want to leave. If she's after the same thing I am—if she has the same knowledge that I do—I wonder what else she knows.

The woman cocks a brow. *As if you could beat me there.*

I wink. *Good luck,* I say, before ducking into the tunnel that led me here.

I don't need luck.

That's the last thing she says to me before I slip out.

CHAPTER 4

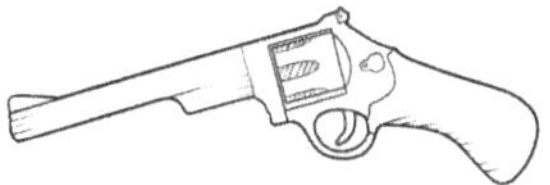

VIENNE

Magic.

I shove the worm into my pocket just as Raiden and the rest of the team appear at the top of the stairs. Raiden has a panicked look on his face, his jaw clenched. Then he spots me down below and his eyes narrow.

"Vienne!" He rushes down the stairs, the rest of the team following him. "We heard a horrible sound, like this place was caving in."

Shit. I have no explanation for that. Still, it's a little charming that Raiden thought I was in trouble and ran to the rescue.

Maybe there's hope for him.

"It was a booby trap," I say off the cuff. "You should've seen it. A big hole opened up in the floor, and these spinning blades came out." I hold one of my hands up, stopping him in his tracks. "You shouldn't come any closer. I don't know where the rest of the triggers are."

I pull out my gun and, feigning that I'm stepping carefully, head toward him and the others. The rest of the team is murmuring apprehensively as I make it to the stairs.

"We should leave," I tell Raiden. "There's nothing down here but traps. I looked all over."

He scowls. "You shouldn't have. Not before we got here. I might have noticed it before it almost killed you."

Aw. He's feeling protective.

"I'm fine!" I spin my pistol before tucking it away. "No problem. But really, we should go. I took some etchings of the writing already so we can compare it with the other carvings we've seen."

Raiden searches my face for a moment with his dark eyes, but eventually, he nods.

"All right. Let's get out of here." He gestures for the others to head back up the way they came. "Step carefully. We don't know what else is down here."

As we head back up to the surface, I throw one more look over my shoulder. That orc... I didn't even get his name.

I wonder who he is. How much he knows. Clearly, far more than I do.

The Stoneteeth Mountains. That's where he's headed next. And if there really is more of that "magic" stuff waiting for us there...

The orc materialized his huge pet lizard out of thin air, as if anything he wanted he could make real. I deeply fear what would happen if that kind of power were to fall in the hands of a wannabe soldier like Raiden.

And I think the orc was right. What would the King do if he found out such a thing existed? The last war raged for my whole life, up until a few years ago, when the conscriptions began and humans and trollkin spilled blood all across the world. I was only spared from serving because I was a part of the History Corps.

It took thousands of deaths for us to finally reach a truce, one made simply because the King and the Grand Chieftain were running out of bodies to throw at each other.

That's all this is: a pause in the violence. There's not peace, and there probably never will be.

I take one last look at the carvings on the wall before I follow Raiden up into the dark, stone tunnel that leads out of here—the human face and the trollkin one, staring into each other's eyes, clasping hands.

It all means something, but what? I wish I could have talked to that orc a little longer. There was something familiar in his eager, curious eyes. He had no weapons on him, and he certainly wasn't afraid of what he might find here, which tells me he hasn't been to many ruins before. But he knew things. He had answers, and I want them.

I leave with far more questions than I had before I ever found this place.

That night, after everyone has gone to bed, I'm lying on my bedroll reading a book when the flap of my tent opens. I know it's Raiden before he even crouches down and reveals his face.

"Hey," he says with a smirk, because usually, I would say, "hey" back in a sultry tone, and then he'd crawl into my tent, take off his clothes, and we'd fuck until one or maybe both of us came—usually just him, though.

Tonight, I couldn't be less interested. My mind is awash with a million other thoughts, all of them about what I saw today, and the orc who spoke inside my head, in my own language.

We could understand each other. This thought repeats over and over again. I spoke to an orc, and he spoke back. He is my enemy, I know this. But for a time, he couldn't have cared less that I was human and he was trollkin. All he was interested in was the past, the world in which the magic came from, and in that way I felt... understood.

"Not tonight," I hiss at Raiden as he starts wriggling into my tent. I put up a hand to stop him, and he gives me a consternated expression.

"What's wrong?" He comes all the way inside, already taking off his shirt. "That booby trap today didn't unsettle you, did it?"

"No!" I snap. "I just don't want to fuck tonight, all right?"

Raiden freezes, gaping at me. That was surprisingly loud, and there's a good chance half of the camp heard me. His hands drop back to his sides, and his brows fall low over his eyes.

"You're sending me away?" he huffs. "You never send me away."

That makes me sound so pathetic—and fuck, maybe I am. Raiden's good looking with his dashing dark hair and chiseled chin, and I liked his attention. It felt great to have it once upon a time, but tonight, I just want to be alone with my questions. Besides, he was the first to send me into that dark ruin alone. Let's just say my flame has been doused, and I want nothing to do with him or his cock.

"Get out, will you?" I push on his chest, knocking him back onto his ass. "This is my tent."

For a brief second, Raiden looks hurt, but then fury clouds his eyes.

"What the fuck, Vienne?" he says under his breath. "You don't have to make me look like an idiot in front of everyone."

"Everyone's asleep. Now go to bed, Raiden."

With a final huff, he steps out, stalking away to his own tent. He'll be salty tomorrow, and he'll probably take it out on me. But I keep thinking about that orc's strange, yellow eyes. His wild, unkempt hair and dirty cheeks, as if all the thoughts in his head are focused on one thing, and one thing alone:

Magic.

It's real, and if I can find my way to the Stoneteeth by myself...

I reach into my pocket, where I shoved the tiny worm before the rock vanished into the ground. When I pull it out, the skin has wrinkled, but the inside still glows purple.

I saw what it's capable of, and that power is as thrilling as it is terrifying. What could I possibly do with it?

I'm still riled up from the day long after Raiden leaves and goes to bed. Usually I use sex to work out my energy and fall asleep, so after tucking the worm away safely, I slide off my pants in my bedroll and reach down between my legs.

I don't need Raiden to get off. In fact, I know that if I do it myself, I have a hundred percent chance of actually coming.

Strangely, as I run my finger in circles around my clit, that damned orc pops back into my mind. He was a big guy, bigger than Raiden by a long shot. I shake my head, trying to clear it as I rub myself harder, faster. Soon my body is seizing, my leg muscles tightening all over as I get closer and closer.

Ah, yes, this is what I needed.

I bite my lip as I finally crest, keeping my moan inside my mouth. It feels as good as I'd hoped it would to release. I lie there panting for some time afterward, staring up at the peaked ceiling of my tent.

I wonder if I'll see that orc again.

GRAZ

I couldn't be more thankful that the human woman understood me, that she grasped just how serious magic is—and how dangerous it would be in the wrong hands.

It's interesting that she was suspicious of her own compatriots. The fear in her clear, blue eyes had been obvious. No, she doesn't trust them, either. It's surprising, but helpful. That's the best outcome I could have hoped for.

Now it begs the question of what I'll find when I reach the Stoneteeth. And in the meantime, I have Izzy with me, which may have been a foolish decision. Now I'm saddled with one grumpy horse and one lazy lizard both.

That night, far from the ruins, I return to my tent and dig out what food I have left. Fuck, I really should go home and restock on things I need. Kalishagg is on the way to where I'm headed, and it's a port city, meaning I can get to the Stoneteeth much faster by ship. Alternatively, I could get on a train and head through the desert, ignoring the open ocean.

Options, options.

I have considered wishing myself places. Of course, that seems like the natural move. Acquire two dozen magic worms, wish myself to the Stoneteeth safely, and not have to travel at all?

I know now what a bad idea that would be. At least Izzy made it safely, but he's still clearly not quite himself. I hope that I haven't hurt him by using magic to transport him, and he comes out of his daze soon.

One lesson learned. The last thing I want is to scramble my own brains.

The next morning, we go back the way we came, and I think Jaks is more than grateful to be heading home. It will take us a week to reach Kalishagg, where I'll check in with the boss and restock. Hopefully I can make it to the next ruin before that human does.

I think about her the whole way home, especially late at night when I'm having trouble sleeping. I don't know if it's fascination or something else, but her wide grin and bright blue eyes both haunt me. Curiosity lit her up in a way that felt familiar, like someone finally understands my fascination.

Now I've shared my secret with another being, and I'm both nervous and relieved. At least I'm not alone any longer in knowing the world is bigger, deeper, and stranger than we all believe.

Unfortunately, that other being was a human.

What if I saw her again? What if I could talk to her again? I want to know everything. Why was she there? Who is she working for?

By the time I reach the high, stone walls of Kalishagg, she's consumed my thoughts, and in more ways than one. She'd been wearing shockingly tight clothing that day, and it showed off her big tits and rather voluptuous hips. Maybe I'm starting to understand what drew Lo'zar to his little human. Their faces are strange without tusks, and their bodies so much weaker and frailer.

And yet, I'm fascinated by the memory of her.

No, I can't go down that road. It's been too long since I got my dick wet, and that's really the problem. I've had some decent fucks before, but nothing serious. When you're involved in Gusak's clan, trollkin come and go often, flitting from one smuggling job to the next.

And besides, none of them have been my mate, so what's the point besides a single night to sate my animal needs?

Maybe it's a foolish hope when so few of us stumble across a true mate in our lives, but I'm holding out. I want what Lo'zar and Rimi obviously had. It was clear as day in their eyes how much they meant to each other—and I want nothing less for myself.

Not that it's so likely for an orc like me. I'm nothing to look at, and I can't seem to ever keep my hair under control. Still my cock is strangely hungry, and I don't think it will stop bothering me until I do something for it.

When I get back to my shop, I'm absolutely exhausted, and feeling the beginning of a headache. Luckily, everything is mostly how I left it. Izzy is eager to see his cage again, as I've been able to find very little for him to eat on the go, and Jaks is happy to be returned to the stable where he can stand there and eat hay all day.

"Graz!" Kugara gasps as she emerges from the elevator that connects my mechanic's shop to the hideout beneath Kalishagg. "You're back!"

I squint as her loud voice makes my pounding headache even worse. She's been much nicer to me since her disastrous episode trying to stop Lo'zar and his mate from leaving the city. He got one over on her and Gusak's other goons during his escape, and even managed to kill one on his way out. I don't blame him, but damn, did it have to be so bloody? It's been tense around here ever since, with Kugara trying to kiss everyone's ass to make up for it.

No one caught wind that I'd helped Lo'zar, thank goodness, or else I'd be dead right now. Gusak doesn't take kindly to those who steal from him, and certainly not to those who shelter said thieves.

He wasn't too kind to Kugara after her failure, either.

"Yup, I'm back." I take off my pack and groan as I set it on the ground. "Fucking exhausted, too."

"Did you find what you were looking for?" She taps the map on the wall.

So Kugara knows what I've been doing. Luckily, it only takes me a moment to come up with a plausible lie.

"Nope," I say, taking off my goggles and smoothing down my hair, though it simply springs back again. "Walked all over, but there's nothing in that damn swamp. I hated it, Izzy hated it, Jaks hated it."

She laughs. "No surprise there. That horse of yours is a grouchy old man." When she spots Izzy on my shoulder, though, she tilts her head. "I thought you'd left your damn lizard, but he went missing a week ago. I thought he'd escaped."

I give her a puzzled look. "I took him with me."

Kugara's brows draw together. "What? I could've sworn…"

I pat her shoulder. "Gusak running you ragged?" He hasn't forgiven her for her fuckup yet, and sends her on one annoying errand after another. "You must be imagining things."

"Must be." She rubs the side of her head. "Damn. I'm too young to be losing my marbles already."

When she's off to do chores in town—which includes picking up some fresh fruit for Izzy—I get into the elevator and head down. I should let the boss know I've passed through in case he needs anything from me.

Unlike the others in the gang, I don't get too deep into Gusak's matters. I don't smuggle for him, though I do funnel his shipments through my shop. I don't steal or lie for him, but I must still play the role of loyal dog if I want to keep my head.

After asking around, I find Gusak in his back room, sitting on a plush couch with an orcess under one arm and a trolless under the other. They're both mostly naked, just a few strips of clothing keeping their tits and cunts hidden. It's not an unusual sight around Gusak, but today I'm even more out of my element than usual.

I have to lie to him—and I've got a pounding headache.

"Ah, it's the bookworm," he says when I appear in the doorway. He beckons me in. "Where have you been?"

I've been working on this particular lie for a while. "I got wind of a tomb out in the swamp."

Gusak sits forward. "A tomb? You didn't tell me."

"I thought I'd investigate first," I hurriedly explain. "Didn't want to waste your valuable time and all."

Gusak snorts. "You're too kind."

"Thought it might be full of riches, but the damned place was empty." I shake my head ruefully. "Nothing."

"Nice try, anyway." He narrows his eyes. "But next time you have a lead, do be sure to tell me."

I duck my head. "Of course."

I won't.

Then Gusak waves a hand dismissively, so I nod and leave.

Thank fuck that went well. But I've always been good at keeping my head down under the powers that be.

Chapter 5

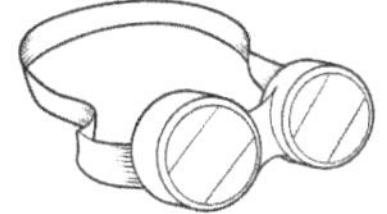

After my brush with Gusak, I meander back out to the massive cavern that the clan calls home. Brightly-colored crystals cover the walls, coming in wild hues of pink and blue and purple, even some green. It's a beauty which hides just how dangerous it is down here. The stone stairs wind around the cavern in a spiral shape, and if you were to slip, you'd tumble down and get speared on a crystal far down below.

The Grand Chieftain doesn't know this is down here, thankfully. Before I came to occupy it, my shop was little more than an abandoned house used as a front for the clan. But when Gusak realized my proclivities were not toward the criminal like my best friend—and I built his elevator for him—he stationed me in the shop to keep an eye on things above ground and disguise his shipments.

There's a campfire going on the third level, so I step off the stairs there to see who might be around home base. An orc I don't recognize sits by the fire eating from a bowl, but his dark demeanor keeps me from greeting him. A young trolless sits on the opposite side, with red hair in a smattering of braids around her head. I think she's one of Gusak's newest recruits, so he keeps her on close missions.

How long ago she was living on the streets? That's how he discovers us, after all, by scooping the dregs of society up off the floor and giving us a place where we can belong.

If you rescue a dog and feed it, you have that dog's loyalty, and he knows that.

"Hey," the trolless says as I squat by the fire near her. "You're the inventor, right?"

I give a disaffected shrug. "Yep."

She sidles a bit closer. "Nice to finally meet you." We shake hands, and hers lingers for much too long on mine.

This would be the perfect opportunity to enjoy a soft cunt and release all this festering hunger inside me. She stays close by as I find something to eat, and makes small talk when I take up residence next to the fire. I'm pretty sure she's interested, which doesn't happen to me often.

But ever since I got back, I have an unbalanced feeling, like my head isn't on straight. And though it's early, I already feel tired. My cock has fallen utterly silent.

Eventually, I get to my feet and say goodbye, much to her disappointment. But she'll find someone else, I'm sure of it. Then I get in the elevator and head back up to my shop.

Besides, I have work to do before I'm ready for my next trip.

Vienne

The entire way back to the King's city of Culberra, Raiden is cold and unyielding. He barks orders at me even when there are more novice recruits among us who should be doing his bidding. There's nothing I can do to get back into his good graces after turning him down, and he makes it known.

I suppose it's what I expected from a military man. His ego is bruised, and now he needs a way to vent his frustration.

I roll my eyes and do what he says when he says it. We may be the History Corps, but we still have our chain of command. It's only another few days until we reach the train, and then we can load up and speed on to Culberra.

Endlessly I play with the withered worm in my pocket, hoping for a moment alone so I can investigate it thoroughly. I fear it as much as I'm dying to learn more about it. It's clearly powerful, if it can grant the ability to communicate across language barriers. And somehow, that orc was able to summon that scaly beast from somewhere else. It appeared like...

Well, magic.

At last, we arrive in Culberra, rolling to a stop at the city station. Raiden goes to meet with the King and discuss our findings, leaving the rest of us free to return home at last.

My apartment is one of four in a small building, and I'm overwhelmed with relief when I open my front door. It's been a month since I was here last, and I can't wait to sleep on my soft bed again, even though it all smells a little dusty.

I enjoy my work with the Corps, and traveling around the world has always been a dream of mine, but that doesn't mean I don't appreciate a down mattress and a feather pillow from time to time.

The moment I lie down, I'm thinking about the worm, about the orc in the ruin and what he was after. Somehow I need to get to the Stoneteeth without Raiden and the rest of the team at my back. I suppose that depending on our next assignment, I could feign illness of some kind, or perhaps put in for a vacation. But I've never skipped a mission, never missed out on an opportunity to go somewhere new and explore the world beyond human territory, and if I did it would certainly make Raiden suspicious.

This is more important than any of the work I've done until now, I know that. Whatever we found in that swamp, it's bigger than the King's History Corps.

I toss and turn all night, unable to quiet my mind. Whenever I close my eyes, I can see that purple glow of magic around the edges of my vision, as if it's closing in on me.

The following day, we all meet to debrief and receive our next assignment. Raiden is rather nasty, and I wonder how long he's going to pick on me before he gets over it. Maybe I should give up and sleep with him again so he leaves me alone.

We all gather around the table, and Raiden relays orders. After finding very little in the swamp, the King's is no longer interested in ancient ruins. Instead, some sailors have discovered an old shipwreck hidden along the coast and he wants us to take stock of it. As always, the unspoken question is whether we'll find some treasure buried inside.

That's what the King is after: rare artifacts, gold, or anything that will translate into wealth. Though he is intrigued by mysteries and new discoveries, which I think is as much entertainment as he gets in his old age. He loves ancient tombs, where kings and queens of the past are buried. He sits, rapt, as Raiden tells him about the offerings we found—with drawn diagrams, of course—and the riches they tried to take with them into the next life. Of course we bring him the loot, too.

I wonder if the King will want to be buried with his wealth. He's long past his prime, so it's not too far off. He's probably considering his own immortality even now.

But the coast is not the direction I want to go; my destination is much farther inland. I know Raiden would never allow me to go do my own investigation, even if I had a plausible reason.

After briefing, the Corps disbands for the night, preparing to leave in two days' time. My mind whirls, trying to think of reasons I could avoid this mission. I sit in my apartment alone in the dark, peering down at the dried-up worm in my hand. It still glows purple inside, as if the worm body is merely a disposable casing for the magic hidden there.

I know I need to be careful with it, whatever it is. I only have one, and who knows when I'll stumble across another?

This ancient civilization, whoever they were, had access to something this powerful. Powerful, but hidden away. So why are they gone now?

I can't keep puzzling over this alone, going around in circles. It's time to go find Mom.

Near where I live—close to the King's castle—the streets are straight and clean, the horse shit quickly cleaned up after it falls. Down in the belly of Culberra, though, things are different. This is where goods are dealt behind closed doors, and children and animals run wild in the filthy alleyways.

This is where the archives are, hidden away in the bottom of the old city.

Now I'm beginning to wish I'd never given Raiden the

information Mom found while she was sorting old books. If they are indeed marking the locations of more magical ruins, it could be a very dangerous thing for him to have. But they were just hunches, legends, about places around the world that ancient people had lived. Hopefully he won't think twice about it after my lie in the swamp.

At last, I reach the archive, which is tucked inconspicuously into a darkened stone doorway. I rap on the heavy wood door and immediately someone calls, "Hold your horses, I'm coming."

It opens with a creak so loud I squint. Mom stands in the doorway, head cocked.

"Vienne!" The deep grooves in her face lift as she smiles. "Come in, come in. You haven't been down in the dregs here for a while."

"Sorry. Went on a long mission."

I can barely see anything when the door to the archives closes behind me, but it's designed this way on purpose. Sunlight would damage much of the collection, so it's all lit by candles.

"How was your trip?" Mom attempts to tidy the mess on her desk, piling papers up haphazardly. "Did you find anything?"

I'm not really supposed to tell anyone about the History Corps's activities, but of course I ignore this direction when it comes to my mother. I sit at the chair across from her on the other side of her desk and lean back.

"Oh, yeah. I found something." I fish the worm out of my pocket and set it on the desk. "I found this."

Her eyes grow huge. Tentatively, she reaches toward it.

"Be careful," I say. "I don't know what it can do."

Mom pauses, because if there's anything I know about my mother, it's that her anxiety of the outside world isn't limited to leaving the archives. Anything foreign or strange makes her quiver.

"What am I looking at?" Mom adjusts her glasses and peers closer.

"Magic, I think."

Her head snaps up. "Pardon me?"

So I recite the whole story from start to finish about the orc I met, about the stone that rose out of the floor, even about lying to Raiden. The wrinkle between her brows grows deeper and deeper.

"Vienne," Mom says in a warning tone. "You are getting into something very serious. Whatever this is, it's beyond dangerous."

I sit up in the chair at the severity of her tone. "What do you think I should do?"

I've always known what I want, always gone after it with relentless abandon. I've crossed oceans and deserts, and Mom has always been the one to temper me, to bring me back to earth and make sure I never end up like my dad. He was also always searching for answers and digging up the past to make sense of it.

He crossed the ocean, intending to do research on the other continent, but his ship vanished. When we never heard word, it was assumed the ship went down in an ocean storm. I never saw him again.

My mother sits in silence for a long time, examining my specimen.

"What if this trollkin you met finds it first?" she says. "What if he's the one you should be afraid of? Maybe it's up to you to go and make sure that doesn't happen—that more magic doesn't fall into the Grand Chieftain's hands."

I couldn't say why, but I feel certain that's not the case. That orc must be a free agent. He was clearly afraid of what would happen if anyone else found out, so I'm nearly certain he's keeping the discovery close to his chest.

"I think you should go to the Stoneteeth." Mom crosses her arms. "As much as I hate to suggest you put yourself in danger by heading into contested territory, you're also the only one I would trust to encounter more magic and do what needs to be done."

I tilt my head. "What needs to be done?"

"Getting rid of it, of course." She gestures with her chin at the worm. "This is immensely powerful, from what you've told me. Should it fall into the wrong hands, it could change the course of the entire world."

I try to imagine what would happen if some asshole like Raiden got his fingers around something like this, and protectively I sweep the worm back up into my hand.

"You want me to destroy it." I tuck it away in my pocket once more. The thought had never occurred to me, but I understand where she's coming from. And maybe she's right. Maybe something like this is from another time, a time when the world was different. Now, given the way things are with war always about to break out, it may be for the best to simply eliminate the threat.

If that's what I need to do, then I also need to get there before that orc does. And that means I have one choice.

When I get home, I start throwing gear into bags, knowing I'll have to leave first thing in the morning. I scribble out a note and address it to Raiden. Partway through, my vision starts to go blurry, but I hastily rub my eyes and finish up, signing my name at the bottom.

It's my resignation letter.

CHAPTER 6

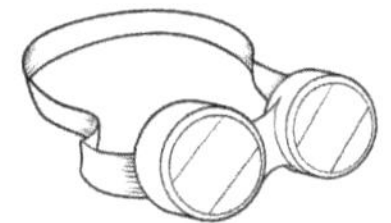

GRAZ

That night, instead of finding my comfort in some soft, rounded body, I sit down with my bag full of shriveled-up worms and examine them closely.

I have so many opportunities right here, so many chances to try new things, that I'm paralyzed by the options. Maybe the first thing I need to do is build myself a translator in case I encounter that human again.

I work late into the night, using the magic I have inside the pendant around my neck. I mimic what I did when I made Lo'zar's necklace, the one that let him appear however he chose, and make my wish: to be able to communicate with humans.

Then, before it can dissipate, I lock it away in the pendant. Now, it's frozen in time, executing my command whenever I need it.

I lock away the bag full of worms in a box in the back of my shop, but stuff one in each pocket in case I need them on the way. Maybe they would come in handy for refueling my supplies should I run out.

Now it's time to go.

I hate traveling.

I hate leaving my shop, where I have everything I need within arm's reach. But I have to get to that second ruin first, in case the human woman comes back with the others in her party.

I know I can't leave again without telling Gusak where I'm going or he might get suspicious this time. The Stoneteeth are a great distance away, and I'll be gone for far longer. I've got to make up some kind of lie that'll make him think I'm looking out for his interests and working toward the betterment of the clan.

When I ask for an audience with him again, I peek into his door to find him poring through rare animal hides.

"Get on with it," Gusak says, not even looking up at me as he leafs through white tiger pelts. One of the pelts vanishes in his hand as he flips it, then reappears when he sets it down again.

"I found another lead." I try not to make myself smaller when Gusak glances up at me. "I was going to pursue it."

"Another one? After the last one was bunk?" Now I've gotten his attention.

Suddenly, the world goes topsy-turvy. I lean against the doorframe to keep from falling over, and Gusak is watching me with even more suspicion in his eyes.

I right myself, unsure of what just came over me, and shrug. "I just... have a good feeling about this one."

Gusak barks out a laugh. "Well, if it were anyone else, I'd

say you were a fool. But you've always been a fool, Graz, and that's what I like about you. So go on your little adventure, and then come back and tell me what you've found."

And like that, I'm a free orc. But I have a feeling if I come back empty-handed again, I might not receive quite so much grace.

The next day, I've packed up my belongings again and said a teary-eyed goodbye to my cot in the corner. Then I'm off, leaving Jaks behind to get on a ship northward. From there I'll take the train, and it won't be more than four days' journey to get where I'm going.

But that morning, I start to feel... strange. Not quite like an illness, but my thoughts are slower than usual and I'm off-balance. I don't know what to make of it.

After boarding the boat heading north, I settle into my cabin to read. Even as I sleep, my vision glows purple at the edges.

Whatever is wrong with me follows me into the next day. I'm sluggish, and yet my skin feels too tight, my nerves frayed and on high alert. I hide out in my cabin except to get meals for the entire journey. When we finally reach dry land, though, I wonder if maybe I was just seasick.

Then I'm boarding the train heading inland. While the Stoneteeth are historically contested territory between humans and trollkin, there are a number of orc towns in the southern part, and that's my first destination. If the human wants to reach the map marker, she'll have to travel lightly and without being seen from the north end to the south. That gives me a good chance of beating her there.

We may be in times of peace, but that doesn't mean she'll

be safe in contested territory. I'm surprised by the twist of my belly at the thought that trollkin might find her and do something awful to her. As much as I don't want her to beat me there, I don't want her to die on the way, either. She has a curious mind, and such a strange, appealing body. The thought of her caught and strung up for mockery fills me with dread.

I'm still feeling unwell as the train stops at my station. I stay overnight at an inn, trying to get my feet under me. My dreams are strange and disturbing, and my sleep is restless.

The next morning, I've managed to shake off some of my fatigue, so I decide to trek off into the mountains. It's slow going with no horse and a big pack, but soon the fresh scent of the mountain air and pine trees calms my rapidly-beating heart.

The first day, I make good progress despite the steep ascent, hiking around massive boulders and following the light trail many others have left behind. This area is ripe for prospecting, and I'm not surprised to find the telltale signs of other travelers. But on the second day, the path diverges. I'm left to make my own way through the dense woods, using the compass to make sure I stay headed the right direction. I plot my progress on the map, using the taller peaks to track how far I've gone and how far I have left to go.

On the third day, my fatigue grows worse. My movement is slow with the persistent fog in my head. Am I more ill than I thought? Should I have stayed behind until I felt better? Will I die out here, and no one will know?

Instead of four days, it takes me five to reach the point on my map where I should find my clue. I'm dragging by now, my pack infinitely heavier than when I left and weighing me down into the dirt. The weather has held despite threats of rain, for which I'm deeply grateful.

After walking uphill all day, at last, I emerge from the trees.

I find myself standing on the edge of a cliff that overlooks the hills below, with no way forward.

Damn it. Really? This is where the map led me?

I curse and stomp one foot, nearly hurling my map off the cliffside. Another dead-end. But the sudden motion has knocked me off-balance, and I stumble back into a sitting position on the ground so I don't tip and fall off the sheer rock face.

That's when I see it. Far down below, on the opposite cliff-side, is a square recess in the rock that is far too perfect and straight to be natural. From what I can make out at this distance, stairs have been carved into the stone leading up from the ground.

That's it. It has to be. Now I've just got to haul myself down there.

Grumbling, I turn around and head back the way I came to search instead for a way off this mountain. I just have to hope that with how tired I am, I don't fall to my death.

Vienne

It feels like I've been hiking these damned peaks for weeks. I've been taking care with my rations, which means I'm hungry—always hungry. I pick nuts when I stumble upon them, but it's getting late in the year, and usually I find nothing but husks when I come across a berry bush. I do manage to shoot a mountain quail one night, and nearly burn myself trying to cook it.

As deep as I am within contested territory, I've tried to move quietly and keep out of sight. My gun stays ready at my hip in case I need it at a moment's notice. I've only encountered two others on my trip so far, and both times, managed to slip off the main path before the big, heavy trollkin coming the other way could stumble across me. I hid until they were gone, then continued on my way, my pack growing lighter with every passing day.

I can smell that I'm close, though. Even though my legs grow tired quickly each day, and my vision is becoming blurry at long distances, I know that I'm going to find what I'm looking for. I keep this at the forefront of my mind as I calculate where I am based on the closest peak, searching for any hint or clue about where an ancient civilization might have built their home.

The next day, I finally make a breakthrough. Deep within the cliffs, along an otherwise innocuous rock face, I spot the shadow of what appear to be stairs.

Rallying what strength I have left, I head down the hillside, picking my way through house-sized boulders and uneven terrain. Usually, I have no trouble scaling a mountainside, but right now my feet might just give out underneath me.

Still, I truck on, because this is what I'm after. This is what I came all this way for.

When I arrive at the foot at the steps, though, a familiar green-skinned orc sits against the cliff wall. He's unmoving, his eyes fixed on some point far in the distance.

I stop a hundred feet away, worried I'll surprise him when he finally notices me. But the closer I get, the less likely it seems. He doesn't react at all as I approach, and now that I'm closer, I can see it: there's a strange purplish glow around the outside of his eyes.

This is... wrong. Whatever has happened to him, it isn't good.

"Hello?" I lean down closer, waving a hand in front of his face. The orc doesn't react—but he isn't dead, either, as his breathing still comes short and shallow. His belongings are scattered all around him, and have apparently been picked through by animals, as if he sat down right here many days ago and hasn't moved since. "Are you alright?"

When there's still no response, my uneasiness grows. He's sick in some way, and I hope it's not contagious.

I probably should leave him here. This could be exactly what I need to keep him out of the way while I do what I came here to do. But he was so excited in that ruin in the swamp, and here he is, merely steps away from his goal and something has stopped him in his tracks.

It would be wrong not to try to help him.

"I need you to get up," I say brusquely. Once more, he doesn't answer. So I reach out and grab his huge, four-fingered hand in mine. *Wake up!* I finally shout with my thoughts. *Get those cobwebs out of your ears!*

It's as if I've cast a magic spell. The foggy sheen across his eyes fades, and the purple hue around the edges dissipates. The orc blinks rapidly, and after a moment, he registers me standing in front of him.

Abruptly, he leaps to his feet, and I stumble back. He mutters something in Trollkin, something I can't understand —but at least he's up and moving again. And he's alive.

I'm filled with immense relief, though I don't know why.

His hair is even wilder than before, his goggles askew. Again he says something in Trollkin, a question, but I have no answers for him.

"Sorry," I say, waving my hands. "I can't understand you."

The orc pauses, then reaches into the collar of his shirt and pulls something out. It's glowing that familiar purple, but the stuff appears to be contained inside of a glass pendant. He holds it out to me, and remembering when we met in the ruin, I reach across the space between us and touch it.

Can you understand me now? a familiar voice asks.

A-ha, there he is. *Yes, I can.*

The orc tucks the necklace away again, and blinking a few times as if to clear away sleep, he scans the area. His brow furrows into a deep crease when he sees his backpack's contents strewn about.

What happened? he asks, perplexed.

I don't know how to explain that he looked like a marionette with the strings cut off, gazing out at nothing. A statue of flesh and blood.

You were just sitting there. I peer closer. *Your eyes. They aren't glowing purple anymore.*

He gapes at me. *Huh? You must be seeing things.*

Whatever it was, it seems like it's gone now.

The orc stretches out his body, testing the movement of his arms and legs.

I was sick, he says at last, surveying his hands. *I think I passed out here.*

I look him up and down. *You don't seem sick anymore.*

I feel... mostly fine. Then he raises his eyes to mine and cocks his head. *You made it.*

I grin as I answer, *I did.*

CHAPTER 7

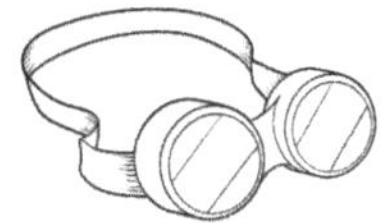

Disturbing, to say the least.

All my food had been devoured by some creature, or perhaps many creatures, and somehow I slept through it all. Now, that human woman is standing right in front of me, her curious blue eyes searching me for clues.

Strangely, I'm pleased to see that she made the journey through contested territory without being caught.

Well, what are we waiting for? she says, planting her hands on her hips. She has a big pack on, and a familiar gun strapped to her hip. I gaze up the steps, then lift each leg a few more times to finish shaking out the stiffness in them.

Lead the way, I say, gesturing for her to go first. Her brows rise, but then she nods. Once I've gathered up what's left of my belongings, she heads off up the stone stairs.

The wall has been rather neatly cut away here, leaving a staircase that's treacherous but stable. I try my hardest as we ascend not to look off to my right, over the empty vastness below.

What's your name? I ask after a time, my breaths coming faster as we continue upward. I need to focus on something besides the height of our climb. I really don't like the steep fall immediately next to us.

The woman pauses, then continues on.

Vienne, she says. *Never thought you'd ask.*

I consider this. *Vienne.* I don't know much about human names, but this seems like a good one.

And you? she asks. *What do I call you, orc?*

I snort. *Graz. Or you can call me "orc."*

She chuckles up ahead of me, tracing the wall of the cliff with one hand as she climbs. *Maybe I'll stick with "orc."*

As we hike, I'm pleased to find my vision has cleared of haze and I can stand up straighter, and though I'm not at my full strength, I have enough in me to keep pace with her. Nothing would be more embarrassing than being shown up by a human.

Vienne hikes on ahead of me, and now that my head has cleared some, I finally grasp what's in front of me. I'd noticed her rather big bosom when we met in the swamp, but I hadn't gotten an eyeful of her rear like I'm getting now. With each stride up the steps, her round ass flexes, and I'm utterly mesmerized by it. Her pants are tight, revealing every curve and crease.

I rub my face, keeping one hand on the cliffside so I don't lose my balance. I can't be ogling a human like this—it's completely disgusting. But even after I pause to get my head on straight, my eyes dart back to each of those two perfect globes in front of me.

Then, abruptly, Vienne slows down. *We're here.*

A small platform waits at the top of the staircase, just big enough for the little human to scoot over and make room for me. Set into the stone are a few steps that lead to a doorway—blocked by a perfectly smooth, flat rock.

We both stare at it for a long time without speaking. We've traveled an immense distance to get here, and now we're faced with nothing but a blank stone wall.

What do we do? Vienne asks, crossing her arms in front of the doorway. *There's no way I came out here for this.*

It does appear decidedly final. There's nowhere else to go, and no obvious way to open it.

Maybe there's a mechanism, I suggest, already poking around the edges of the apparent door for any sign of how it might open. *Like in the swamp.*

Curious, Vienne leans over me, intrigued as I search the floor. But there's no sign of any way to move the massive rock blocking our path.

Well, what if it's done the same way? She reaches one hand out and places it flat on the door. *Remember?*

Right. One human hand and one trollkin hand were required. Perhaps the same will work here, too.

Instead of answering, I press my own palm to the stone beside hers. My green hand with four fingers dwarfs her tan, five-fingered one. I have a stray thought that I like her little hands with the dirty fingernails.

Then, we hear a rumbling. The stone underneath us shakes, and Vienne screeches as she loses her balance. The platform is small, and as she teeters backward, a horrible vision flashes through my mind of her stumbling off the side. I hastily reach out and grab her by the hand, tugging her forward again—which has the side effect of throwing her into me.

I stumble down the steps, into the shallow nook made by the doorway, and hold her tight so she can't fall. All of her curves press into me, and now I am fully aware of just how she's shaped.

Thank you, Vienne says, clinging onto me in return as the earth rumbles underneath us.

I'm about to answer that it was a split-second decision, but then beside me... the rock begins to move.

We both jerk away as the stone blocking the doorway scrapes and groans, slowly parting from the wall. Vienne reaches for her gun, as if some sort of creature inside might spring out and attack us. I'm riveted as a dark space is revealed.

Finally, the doorway is fully exposed, and the shaking ceases. On the other side is a dark stone tunnel, leading deeper into the cliffside. Vienne points her gun inside and, before I can say a word, steps in front of me, as if whatever we might encounter, she's more equipped to handle it than I am.

What are you afraid of? I ask her with a chuckle. *A flesh-eating mummy?*

She leads the way, clicking off the safety on her gun. *You never know what's behind a locked door.*

VIENNE

Snakes, spiders, scorpions—they're all just as likely of threats as booby traps are. I've encountered looters and treasure hunters in old tombs, and I've been forced to defend myself. This guy clearly hasn't been inside that many dark, ancient ruins if he's not more afraid right now.

There's a rustling behind me, and I find Graz kneeling on the ground, rifling through his bag. He withdraws the lamp I saw him carrying last time, and he lights it with a fire starter.

Ready, he says, holding it up.

Nice gadget.

His face flushes a dark green. *Thanks. Made it myself.*

I suppose we're doing this after all, and we're doing it together. I just hope I don't have to hurt him to do what I set out to do here.

At least I'm the one with the gun.

With the additional light, I can make out the shape of a hallway carved into the stone that leads directly into the mountain. As we go deeper, I make out writing along the walls that now looks familiar to me.

I took all the etchings to my Mom to see if she could make sense of it, I say as we walk along the hallway, trailing my fingers over the black markings.

Your mother?

She's an archivist, I say. *She loves this kind of stuff, like figuring out dead languages.*

So far, this place is empty, not a single skittering beetle to be found. We must be deep in the mountain as we progress.

Sounds like an interesting woman. Graz pauses. *Wait. Look.*

Up ahead, there's light—faint purple light. A very familiar purple light.

Magic.

We both hurry our steps, and I don't know if it's because we're both excited or if we're racing to see who can get there first. But Graz's legs are longer than mine, and he makes it to the end of the hallway before I do.

He comes to a sudden stop, and I fall in place beside him when I see it, too.

Spread out below us is a huge open cavern, with a waterfall on the opposite side flowing down into a pool at the bottom. The purple glow emanates from carvings all over the walls, the grooves filled with magic. Jackpot.

I could just jump for joy that my trip here has paid off. I didn't come all this way for nothing. But then I remember what Mom and I talked about, and my blood cools. What will this orc do with it now that we've found it? This is a great and terrible power. Our peoples might be at a truce right now, but this discovery could lead to incredible bloodshed.

Wow, Graz says with wonder in his voice as he gazes around us at the glowing carvings. *What is this place?*

Moss and vines hang down from overhead, as if somewhere high above there's sunlight. In the center of the huge cavern stands a tall pedestal with a broad stone top. It appears to be the only feature besides the glowing carvings—which are all surprisingly familiar.

There are two faces, just like before. On one wall, a human and a trollkin gaze at one another, their hands clasped. On the other side of the waterfall, though, there's more. A small human body is pictured alongside a larger, trollkin one, their limbs tangled up together.

What are they supposed to be doing?

Some kind of ritual site, maybe? I ask as we look down over the cavern. *I've never seen anything like this.*

Graz nods. *You might be right. I wonder what sort of ritual.*

I start down the stone steps toward the floor, still holding my gun.

What about the rest of your group? Graz asks, making me pause. *Where are they?*

It takes a moment to register what he means. He's asking about Raiden and the others, who I left behind without even telling them where I was headed.

They're not here. It's just me. I spread my arms wide. *So if you want to kill me, no one will know where to look, and no one will find my body.*

I mean it as a joke, but it's certainly possible he'll just push me off the stairs and call it good. I've probably made a mistake in trusting him so far, but as usual, I've let my curiosity get the better of me.

Graz narrows his eyes, like he's suspicious of my motives, too. And I suppose he has no reason to trust me, given who we are and where we come from. Just like I worry he'll hand over the source of magic to the Grand Chieftain, which would rain down hell on his human enemies, wiping out my entire civilization—he could very well be dreading the same thing.

If the King got his hands on this, he would eviscerate the trollkin. Wipe them off the face of the land.

The orc studies me, and I can't figure out what he's thinking behind those yellow eyes with the amber irises. Perhaps he is weighing the scales, too.

All right, he says at last, gesturing for me to head down the stairs. *You go first.*

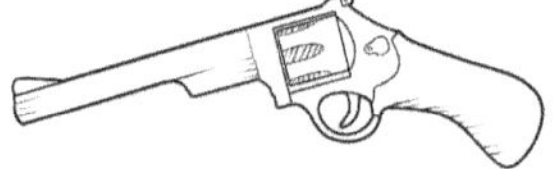

VIENNE

I descend the steps deeper into the cave, Graz close behind. It's humid in here from the waterfall, and droplets cling to the stone walls. No wonder there's so much moss growing in here.

Graz is tracing every last inch of the carvings, trying to suss out what they mean. We haven't found a pair of matching handprints here like we did in the swamp. I think that the pedestal is important, given that it features in one of the carvings, but I don't know what to make of the two bodies on top of it.

When we reach the bottom, we both stand in front of the design, studying it. Then Graz moves on and I follow him to the other side of the cave to inspect the other one, too. I walk up to it and run my hand along the groove, thinking I might be able to touch the magic woven inside it, but my hand comes away clean. Even when Graz places his hand alongside mine, nothing happens.

There's nothing else down here, I say, annoyed. *I came all this way for some more drawings on the wall?*

Graz shakes his head. *There has to be something here. I just think it's hidden.*

But how do we open it this time? I ask. There's nothing obvious, even after I've searched the entire floor of the cavern. The only thing here is that damned pedestal in the middle.

What does it mean?! I let out a frustrated sound and squat down on the floor. Then I remember I still have one of those magic worms left in my pocket. *Oh! Do you think this would help?*

I pull it out and hold it up. Graz reaches into his own pocket to pull one out, too.

We can try, I guess, he says. *I don't think it could hurt if we're careful with what we ask.*

What about... show us what it means?

Sure. He gets a mischievous smile on his face. *I've never tried something so esoteric. We'll see what happens.*

So I stand up, holding the worm out in my hand, and make my wish: *Show me what this means and what we're supposed to do.*

The magic inside the worm glows brightly, growing and growing, until suddenly it winks out.

Absolutely nothing happens.

We exchange looks. I think that's the last thing we expected.

Hmm. Must have wished for the wrong thing, Graz says.

What would you wish for? I shoot back.

He just smirks at me. *Something else. Maybe... open up?*

Simple enough. I do feel a little silly for not thinking of it myself.

He holds up one of his own worms, closes his eyes, and his mouth mutters words I don't understand. Like mine, the magic inside his glows brighter and brighter until it abruptly goes dark.

And still, there's nothing. Though the purple inside the grooves of the carvings seem to glow a little brighter, that's it.

Damn it. I smack a fist against the wall of the cavern. *I came all this way!*

This magic, Graz says gesturing at the wall. *This has to mean something. I'm sure ancient people knew.*

I sigh and roll my eyes. *Maybe. But what is the wall telling us?*

I can't say I know the answer to that.

We both start searching again for some hidden panel, some way to reveal the secret of this cavern.

I'm exhausted, Graz finally says after he's traversed the entire edge, examining every carving and drawing. He sits down, rocking forward to drop his head into his hands. *Whatever happened to me out there, it sapped all my energy.*

Right. I think of all his eaten food, when clearly the visiting animals hadn't woken him.

What happened to you, anyway? I ask.

I couldn't tell you. I started feeling sick a while back, and it only got worse. However long I was out... I don't remember any of it.

I was sick, too. Now that I think about it, I feel better now than I have since I arrived in the Stoneteeth. *But not anymore, it seems like.*

Graz's eyes travel up the cavern wall to the domed ceiling, shrouded in darkness. He slowly turns to me, tilting his chin down so he can look me in the eyes. *You were able to wake me up.*

I guess so, but I don't know how. I shrug. Maybe I was just in the right place at the right time. *You should get some rest. And tomorrow, you'll be thinking more clearly.* I could use a good sleep, too, after how long I've been traveling.

Graz grunts. *That might not be a bad idea.*

He heads to his pack and pulls out his bedroll, and I do the same. We arrange ourselves not too close to each other, then Graz puts out the light.

When I awaken, it's to the sound of many, many voices. They're all speaking animatedly, but in a language I can't understand.

I sit up, panicked, to find myself sitting on the cavern floor without my bedroll. The voices are coming from people all around me, people I've never seen before, dressed in leather tunics and loincloths. Their legs box me in, and I let out a cry as someone gets so close to me they almost step on me.

Vienne?

I glance around at the sound of Graz's voice. Where is he?

Graz? I try to stand up despite the mass of bodies. Not far away, though many people fill up the distance between us, I spot Graz's tall, wild hair and green skin. Though there are mostly humans around me, when I rise to my toes to get a better look, I find there are trollkin here, too, in a variety of green, blue, and purple hues.

I push my way through the crowd toward Graz, and he reaches out to me, grabbing my hand. No one around us seems to even notice our presence.

Where are we? I think frantically. *Who are these people?*

I don't know. He doesn't let me go as we're pushed about by other bodies, coming at us from every direction. He pulls me against him so I'm not swept away.

Then, suddenly, a horn sounds. Everyone stops moving all at once, and their voices drop into silence.

Graz and I turn in unison as we catch sight of movement. Two figures are being lifted up onto the massive pedestal in the center of the room—one human man, and one trollkin woman with purple skin and purple hair.

They're both completely naked. I gape openly as they stand up on the top of the pedestal, their hands linked. A wild cheer goes up from the assembled people, humans and trollkin alike waving their arms and roaring. The two participants on the pedestal bow together as if they're about to put on a play, and then turn to face each other.

The human trails his hand down the troll woman's side, smoothing it over the swell of her breasts to her thick thighs. Silence falls again when he grips one and she sags toward him, as if this is an intimate dance they've danced before.

But now, we are all watching.

What's going on? I ask Graz, unwilling to pull away even though we're uncomfortably close. I'd rather be in his bubble than near all these mysterious strangers. *Where did all these people come from?*

I have no idea. He peers around at the humans and trollkin alike crammed in tight. *They're dressed strangely, too.*

He's right. They look like they're from another time, before we invented textiles.

Up on the pedestal, a harsh moan captures my attention. The human is now plucking the troll woman's nipples, his hand wrapped around one breast while he leans down to lick the other.

Graz...? I ask with deep uncertainty. *What are we looking at?*

He says nothing as the two performers continue. His eyes are riveted to them, his mouth slowly opening. I follow his gaze to where the troll woman has spread her legs, and the man kneels between them to bury his mouth in the crux of her thighs. The troll lets out a pleased whimper, and murmurs spread throughout the crowd.

Then the man pulls the troll woman down onto the

pedestal with him, and his cock is hard and thick. He positions himself with her knees to either side of him, and I cover my mouth.

He's going to do it. Right here, in front of everyone. I squeeze Graz's arm tighter. Why are all these people watching this?

Why are *we* watching this?

The man plays with the troll's pussy, smearing himself all over her before he finally sinks his cock inside her. I gasp, while the people gathered around us hoot and holler.

The troll woman moans as he buries himself deep, then pulls out of her again. They fuck like that, her arms winding around his neck while I stare, unable to tear my eyes away. I'm getting warm all over just watching them, at the sight of them staring into each other's faces as if none of us are here while he pumps his cock in and out of her.

Graz grips me tighter, too, keeping me close at his side and away from the others with one arm curled around my back.

Now both of them are moaning, the troll woman's legs curling around the man's hips as he drives in, the slap of their bodies filling the air. The troll throws her head back, crying out as the man fucks her harder, the muscle of his ass flexing with every thrust.

It is, bizarrely, beautiful.

Graz

Oh, I am definitely getting a boner. An absolute raging hard-on, watching this human man plowing a trolless until she's screaming something incomprehensible. And Vienne, with her gun in the holster, is gripping me like I'm her last lifeline. I'm tingling every place we're touching, all along the arm that's wrapped around her shoulders, and the other arm that she's holding onto tightly.

The entire time, I'm sporting a tent.

Where did all these people come from? While enraptured with the event on the pedestal, I'm still trying to piece it together. It's as if a whole civilization appeared out of thin air. A civilization where humans and trollkin live side-by-side.

This can't be real. Whatever we're seeing, perhaps that sickness has truly taken hold of us both. Is this the actual Vienne next to me, or just a figment of my imagination? Am I dreaming?

If it were my dream, though, she'd probably be wearing fewer clothes. It's impossible not to imagine it while this goes on in front of us.

Up on the pedestal, the trolless cries out her ecstasy as the man plunges into her again and again. And then, as their cries climb in volume, the base of the pedestal begins to glow. Purple light emanates out from around it, billowing up brighter and brighter as the two pursue their climaxes. Soon, it looks like they are beings of pure light moving in unison.

There's no question in my mind, looking at them, that they're mates. The man guides his face lower, so their noses are touching as they both, at last, reach their finish.

The stone pedestal creaks as the light grows brighter, and then it begins to rise. The trolless and the human man are both panting as they ascend into the air, and beneath them, the pedestal reveals a pool of bubbling, glowing magic down below.

Everyone around us falls to their knees as the pool is exposed, leaving the two of us standing there. None of them reach out to touch it—they all keep a safe distance. We are ignored, as if we aren't even there.

After only a few moments, they rise to their feet again, and at once they turn around to leave. And then, everything goes dark.

Whether I wake up only seconds or many hours later, I have no way of knowing. My eyes snap open and I sit up, wrapped up in my bedroll as if I've been tossing and turning all night. Beside me, I hear Vienne's labored breathing, and turn to find her gaping at me.

I don't need to ask to know that we *were* both there. We saw the same thing.

Did we cause that with our wish?

And now we're back here again, completely alone. The cave looks much different, too. In our dream—or vivid hallucination, it's a matter of taste—there was no moss decorating the walls, no vines hanging down from the ceiling, no ivy creeping along the rock faces. It's likely that hundreds, maybe thousands of years, have passed since this cave looked the way it did in our dream.

Are all those humans and trollkin who gathered here dead now? Were they ever real at all?

That happened, right? Vienne asks, still frozen in her bedroll. *Did you see it, too?*

I nod. *Clear as day. That was... something.*

Her mouth bobs open like she's going to speak, but then she closes it again. Her whole face turns red and her gaze darts away from mine.

Ah. Right. I still have a hard-on under my pants that I'm hiding with my own blanket.

There's magic hidden under there. She gestures at the pedestal in the center of the cavern.

If it was there once upon a time, what's the chance it's still there now? Finally abandoning my bedroll, I creep over to the pedestal to investigate. Sure enough, there's a seam along the floor where it detached and rose, but there's no sign of anything down beneath it.

I think it's there, Vienne insists. *If we can figure out how to open it.*

She joins me, standing rather close to my side as we both inspect the ritual site. But my thoughts keep gliding back to what we saw up there, how that trolless and her human lover appeared to have summoned it through their coupling.

That can't possibly be the trigger—except that vision was appallingly clear. I know what we have to do.

CHAPTER 9

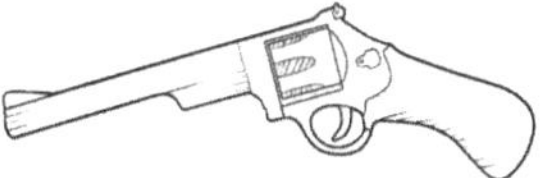

VIENNE

I think the orc and I have come to the same realization.

That scene we witnessed... it must have been some echo of the past. I don't know how or why, but I suspect it has something to do with magic. We were *meant* to see it.

Perhaps that was how our wishes came true.

We stand next to each other in silence, neither of us willing to say it aloud. There's no way I could do such a heinous thing with an orc, even if that's what it takes to reveal the mystery of this place. And damn, do I want those answers.

Graz clears his throat.

If we can figure out how to open it, he repeats, his gaze flicking over to me and then back at the pedestal.

I shiver. Surely there's another way. I drag over my bag and kneel to pull out a pickaxe. I slip the pick end through the crack around the base of the pedestal and, with all my might, I try to pry it open.

I don't think that's going to work. Graz stands with his arms crossed as the wooden handle flexes to the point of breaking.

Then what do you suggest? I ask. Surely he's against the idea of us doing... whatever that man and that troll woman did.

The orc is silent, though, so I continue trying. Eventually, though, the metal begins to give, and I have to give up or risk snapping it.

I drop my pickaxe to the ground, panting. Graz crouches beside me, surveying the juncture closely. It really does look like there's only one way to summon whatever is underneath here.

We have to do it, I say eventually, my voice catching. I can't believe I'm even saying this.

His head snaps up, his eyes narrowing on my face. *You can't be serious.*

It's either that, or we leave without knowing what this place is or what those carvings mean. And as much as I fear what we might find, I can't stand the idea of coming all this way just to leave the mystery unsolved.

Graz growls. *Then we're leaving*, he says with a certainty.

I frown. Am I really so bad to look at? Well, by trollkin standards, I might not be a spring chicken. I'm small, smaller than that troll woman, and shaped quite differently.

We could close our eyes, I suggest.

No. Graz's face is a dark shade of green at the cheeks, and he seems committed to staring at the carvings on the wall. *Absolutely not.*

I rise to my feet, insulted but not surprised. I'm human and he's trollkin. What we saw up there? It should be disgusting to me, to have seen that.

But it wasn't. It was... strangely lovely. There was something between them that transcended us onlookers, as if we weren't even in the room.

Graz doesn't seem even remotely close to budging, though. I'm going to have to wait him out, or see if he comes up with something better.

After a while I grow bored waiting for him to come up with a better plan, so I head to the pool to drink water. I'm filthy all over, and though it's ice cold, it might put some life back in me again to bathe—and maybe I'll get a grand idea while I do it.

You're going to do that? Now? Graz asks as I unbutton my shirt.

What? I'm filthy.

That's true.

I scowl at him over my shoulder, but Graz just shrugs.

I ignore him as I take my clothes the rest of the way off, and he turns his back to me. Then I slide into the frigid pool.

Quickly and efficiently, I wash up as best I can with just my hands, wiping off all the grime and sweat from the journey. When I'm finished, I'm squeaky clean and shivering. I sit down on a rock and shake my arms out, trying to get the water off of me so I can put my clothes back on without drenching them.

I can hear your teeth chattering all the way over here, Graz grumbles. *You shouldn't have gotten wet.*

At least I'm clean.

He lets out a heavy sigh, his back still facing me. *I don't know why you want to do this.*

I trekked all the way through these fucking mountains for answers, and I'm going to get them. I even gave up my job.

His brows rise in surprise. *Your job? Really?* Then his shoulders curl forward. *I've seen it before, you know.*

Seen what, a human and a troll fucking? You've been to some wild parties.

He doesn't answer right away. Then he says, *It was my best friend. He's a troll, and he found a human mate.*

A mate? What's that?

Graz lets out a chuckle. *It's everything. Your whole world. The reason for existing.*

I think about that. Sounds like a bigger deal than just marriage.

You think that's what the man and the troll were? I ask. *Mates? Couldn't you see it in their faces?*

I have to admit that what we saw didn't look ordinary. There was some kind of energy radiating off of them, something not quite of this world when they looked into one another's eyes.

You really know of this happening before? I ask. *Your friend?*

Graz nods. *Saw it with my own eyes. A human and a troll, absolutely crazy about each other.*

So crossing the lines in the sand between our civilizations isn't as out of the ordinary as I'd thought. And it's becoming clearer and clearer that's what these carvings are saying—it'll take both of us, one human and one trollkin, to make this work.

We have to try something. I stand up, still naked, and approach the pedestal. It's high up, so I have to hop to get onto it.

Maybe this orc isn't as bad to look at as I feared. Sure, his hair is a little out of control, but he's muscled in all the right ways. And if his body is that big, then...

What are you doing? Graz asks, finally turning to look at me. His mouth falls open when he sees me sitting there, as naked as the day I was born.

What I have to do to get to the bottom of this. I lean forward, bracing my hands on my thighs. *Or would you rather leave and never find out the truth?*

He scowls. *Those are the options? There has to be another way.*

GRAZ

What she's asking is, by all accounts, ridiculous. Unhinged, like a door missing a screw. There's a pair of misaligned gears in her head. Those are the only explanations for a small woman with a straw-colored bob of hair and bright, sapphire eyes sitting naked on a raised pedestal, offering herself up to me.

I think.

The worst part is that I should, by all accounts, detest the idea of this. I should loathe the image of soiling myself with a human the way that Lo'zar did. I should tell her that there's no curiosity in the world, no secret worth this.

But I don't. The sight of her pink nipples resting atop surprisingly round breasts isn't unappealing. Her cunt is hidden beneath light brown hair, but her thighs are broad and strong, her small feet adorned with five tiny toes.

I wonder what it would be like to lick them.

Shaking my head, I advance a step toward her. I can always close my eyes while I do it. She may not be my mate, but this could be our only way in. Perhaps if I treat it like every other time I've done the deed simply to sate my needs.

Well? Vienne asks, cocking a brow. *Are you going to try to do it all dressed up like that?* She gestures with her chin in the direction of the water. *Maybe you could take a bath.*

I grumble. I don't want to get frigid cold, too, but it would be rather unpleasant of me to climb on top of her after I sat at the base of the cliff in a stupor for who knows how long.

Fine. Give me a moment. Eyeing her warily, I make my way over to the pool of water, knowing it's going to be so cold it'll shrink my balls. Exactly what you want to have happen at a moment like this. Definitely.

As expected, it's like diving into ice, but I dunk my head under and scrub my hair, then make sure to get everywhere else that might be stinky and dirty. I pay special attention to getting my cock clean, all while I'm thinking about what's going to happen once I step out of this water.

Am I really thinking about this? Am I truly considering doing it?

Don't worry, Vienne says. *We'll get warm again.*

When I look up, she has a smirk on her face—almost like she's anticipating what's going to happen next, and I wonder what she thinks of me. Does she like what she sees, or does she think me disgusting?

You know, I can hear your brain whirring even when you're quiet, she says, crossing her legs neatly on the pedestal. *It never stops, does it?*

I shake my head as I climb out, leaving my goggles where they are on the cavern floor with my clothing.

No. Or at least, I don't think so. There's always a problem to solve.

She nods as I get nearer, water sliding down my body and leaving chilly trails behind. But the longer I look at this woman, the closer I get to her, the more the cold isn't bothering me. Instead, I'm wondering what those cute little nipples might feel like, as tight and hard as they are. I wonder if they'd warm up in my mouth.

I'm surprised at myself. But if this is what I have to do today, then I'm not displeased to enjoy it.

I climb up onto the pedestal, joining her. Vienne's eyes search me, from my face down to my chest, then to my cock. She doesn't hide her expression at all.

Oh. Okay. She licks her lips, and I can't tell if it's a nervous gesture or a hungry one. *That's what we're working with.*

I follow her gaze to where I'm slowly starting to thicken

and rise at the groin. It probably looks strange to her. But that human man didn't have that different of anatomy, just—

Right. Vienne is a tiny woman and I'm much bigger. I'll have to be careful with her.

I don't know how to start this, but I think anything I do will be awkward, so I close the distance between us and reach for her breast first. I'm startled by how warm she is now, how soft and incredibly round it is in my palm.

She gives me an odd look. *That's it?*

I guess I am just standing here with a hand on her tit. I need to take control of this situation somehow and warm her up for me, but I've never tried to fuck a human before.

What the hell am I doing?

I push Vienne back onto the pedestal, and she lets out a squeak as her bare back touches the stone. Sighing, I climb up onto it, and crouching over her, curl one arm underneath her to keep her off the cold, wet rock. Her eyes widen as I retake her breast in my hand, then lower my mouth to wrap around her nipple.

Vienne lets out an exclamation in her language as I seize onto it, lapping over the tiny pebble with my tongue. Then I suck again, the way a whelp would, and my cock jolts between my legs when she gasps. This is a good start.

When I'm finished attending to one nipple, I switch to the other, nursing it with my lips and tongue. Vienne's back arches into me—another good sign. This time, I gently run my teeth over the tip, gauging whether she likes it.

A moan falls from her lips. I do it again, then soothe the nipple with my tongue, and she rises even higher off the pedestal.

Do you like that? I ask, grinning as I suck harder. *Does that turn you on?*

Y-yeah. Her answer is uncertain, but I don't think her body is uncertain.

Maybe I can have fun with this after all.

CHAPTER 10

VIENNE

I don't know what I thought was going to happen, but I didn't expect him to start this way. The orc is lavishing attention on my breasts, nipping and licking and sucking them like a professional. He's naked on top of me, and I feel it the moment his cock nudges at my thighs.

Damn. That thing is *big*. When Graz got out of the water naked and I saw it... I was thrilled and afraid at the same time. The tip appears to be wet, too, because I feel moisture drag over my thigh, leaving a smear behind as Graz squeezes one breast in his hand and plucks my nipple with his teeth.

I can't help but moan at the combination of pleasure and pain. His eyes shoot up to mine at the sound, and his pupils are huge and black, his brows lowered in concentration. Our gazes remain locked as he weaves his hand down my belly, smoothing his palm over the skin like he's testing out the feel of me.

Raiden certainly never did this much foreplay, and here's an orc showing him up.

In turn, I sample the texture of Graz's arms underneath the hair that covers his chest, arms, and legs. Then I run my hands to his broad shoulders and his thick neck. It isn't obvious how big he is when he's at a distance, but right here on top of me, it's impossible not to notice the size of him, just how much muscle is packed underneath that green skin.

Graz is still staring at me as he explores farther south, down between my legs. I spread them for him, because I know where this needs to go, and a smile plays at the edge of his mouth.

Are you excited? he asks, running his finger through the hair at the juncture of my thighs. I wriggle, waiting for him to go lower. *Do you want me, little human? Do you want an orc to fuck you?*

I know I shouldn't, but all I want is the next step, the following page, the final act. Graz releases my breast, rising up over me on the pedestal with his cock alert, waiting for my answer. But I've already thrown caution to the wind and left the Corps. Besides, who's he going to tell? Raiden's on the coast somewhere hunting for treasure. No one can see me but this orc.

Graz peers down at me, his hand just inches away from where I want it to be.

Yes, I answer. *Are you going to touch me now, or what?*

That tickle at the side of his mouth erupts into a smug smirk. This guy has an attitude on him.

He slides his palm lower, finally coasting the pads of his fingers over my sex. His brow lifts, and he leans down closer.

You're wet. His voice is low, even in his thoughts. *Did it turn you on that much?*

I grit my teeth because I know what he wants, and I'm not going to give him compliments.

Don't worry, he says. *I'll make you sing soon enough.*

Then he sinks his finger into me. It's just the tip, just exploratory, but he's right—I'm wet and I'm excited. He drags it upward, right over the tip of my clit, which makes me gasp and twitch. Graz lowers his lids as he does it again, gently brushing over me, and my hips jerk. He cups my pussy in his hand, dipping his finger inside me again to soak it in my wetness.

He's slow and methodical about his teasing, which is slowly driving me mad—winding me up, one little touch at a time, urging me from one flight of stairs to the next. All with his hand.

Raiden couldn't dream.

I'm about to erupt when suddenly, Graz slows down, and rubs his fingers up and down my swollen outer lips. But I'm desperate now, craving so much more.

Why did you stop? I demand.

Graz chuckles, then pushes my legs wider. He creeps downward, and I squeak as he hooks his hands under my thighs.

Wait, what are you doing? I don't know why I'm asking the question when it's perfectly clear where he's headed. He's going to eat me out, when there's really no need for that. I thought we just had to have sex for this to work.

Damn. The orc huffs in a deep breath, and his eyes look even more blown-out than before. *You smell... incredible.*

What?! I reach down to push him away, but I'm too late. Graz shoves his face between my legs, licking from my seam all the way up to my clit, which he ravenously circles, then slurps up between his lips.

I've never, ever had someone go down on me like this

before, and I'm entranced. He's licking every part of me, exploring it with his tongue, reaching inside me with it and pressing everywhere, and that steady ache he'd been building in me earlier billows up into a flame.

Oh, fuck, I think, and it's the last two coherent words that come out of me. That tongue and those lips are whipping me into a storm, a whirling dervish that grows wilder with each passing second.

Then, a sturdy finger presses inside me. I'm so wet that it goes through easily, slipping between the lips of my pussy. The invasion is surprising and deliciously welcome, and my hips buck as he thrusts it in deep.

Graz moans against my clit, pausing momentarily in assaulting it.

So small, he says, his thoughts coated with lust. *And sopping wet.* His finger withdraws, then slides back in, matching the tempo of his mouth. *Do you like getting eaten out by an orc?*

Yes! I don't want him to stop. *Yes, I do!*

He grunts with satisfaction, licking faster, thrusting faster. I'm startled when the lightning bolt strikes me, spreading from where Graz is sucking me dry up my spine and into my arms and legs. I can't help but cry out, my thighs squeezing tight around his head even as he continues fucking me with his tongue and fingers, extending my finish as far as he can.

That's fucking delicious, Graz announces when he lifts his head, his hand sliding out of me with an obscene sound. *I've never had anything like it. Every perfect meal put together.* His eyes are glittering, like he's just experienced something that's changed his life forever.

Graz crawls upward until he's fully surrounding me, bracketing me with his huge arms. The big orc is panting, his face soaked. I've never seen someone go so absolutely wild on pussy before.

Holy hell. I reach up to touch his cheek. He looks so strange, so different with those big tusks of his and his yellow eyes—but I think that perhaps, he's also beautiful.

Or is that just because he ate me out like I was his last meal? I must be drunk on it.

Graz leans down so his face is much closer to mine, his hot breath gusting over my cheeks. His expression is oddly vulnerable, like he's awaiting my judgment. His lips are parted, and they're thick and full as they wrap around his tusks. His eyes are heated, but still he hovers, like he's afraid of the next step.

But now I want nothing more. The ripples of my orgasm finally ebb, leaving me even more needy, even more empty than before.

So I raise my head, fueled by pure need and instinct, and press my lips to his.

GRAZ

Oh. All right.

She's kissing me, and for too long I sit there, stunned. I didn't expect this to become, well, intimate.

Then Vienne pulls back, licking her lips awkwardly. Her cheeks are a perfect blush pink.

Sorry, she says.

But I liked it. I liked it quite a bit. I lower myself on my elbows, our bodies pressing together on the pedestal.

Her uncertainty grows. *I didn't mean to—*

Interrupting her, I smash my mouth against hers. Vienne's lips open in surprise under mine, and I take the opportunity to lick the lower one. When I nibble it with my teeth, her whole body jolts underneath me, her breasts pushing enticingly into my chest.

My cock is roaring for attention, so I grind it against her hips, the fur between her thighs tickling the shaft as I kiss her harder. The idea of burying it inside this small woman is no longer a horrifying idea, but one I'm ravenous for. And besides, no one who would judge me will ever know.

It's as if all of my senses have heightened. Now I can smell her, and it's absolutely intoxicating all around me. Her skin, still cold from her bathing, is blissfully soft under my hands as I grip her hips. I can hear each one of her gasping breaths in my ears and in my mouth as I push her lips apart, then explore with my tongue. Hers is waiting for me, and the taste of her...

Even more of my blood flows into my groin. I don't know how much more of this I can take. Then, I remember I can still kiss her while I'm inside her, and I break away to breathe in air. Vienne's cheeks are hot and red, her lips swollen, her blue eyes as big and deep as the sky. I could drown in them.

I reach down between us, remembering just how small she was when I slipped my finger inside her. I hope that she can open up for me.

Finding her even wetter than before, I'm immensely pleased as I push that finger in again, circling it inside her until I manage to slip a second one through. She squeezes artfully around me, her eyelids drifting to half-mast. A moan rewards me as I explore deeper, spreading her wider.

I think she wants my cock, and that's the most marvelous prize of them all.

Biting my lip to keep my snarling instincts at bay, I pump my hand faster, spreading my fingers apart to open her for me. Vienne's little body clenches, her hips jerking against me with each movement. I'm already leaking for her, ready to cover her with my seed.

At last, I'm able to fit three fingers inside her, and now I think she's ready. She bites into her lip, squeaking.

Just getting you prepared for me, I assure her, twisting my hand and thrusting it faster. She's so slick that they easily move, and I can feel the delightfully soft texture of her cunt with each stroke.

It's time.

VIENNE

I know what Graz is doing, and it's wise since I've seen just how well-endowed he is. Perhaps he's normal for an orc, but I've never seen an orc's cock before, so I have nothing to compare it to.

Are you ready for me? he asks in a thick voice. We're both starving now, and I dig my fingers deep into the green flesh of his arms as he withdraws his hand from between my legs.

Do it. My body lifts toward his as if drawn by a magnet. *Give me everything.*

With a sturdy grunt, Graz sits back on his thighs and grabs my legs, pulling them apart. He strokes himself as he gazes down at me, eclipsing the green head of his cock with his fore-skin, then pulling it away again to leave the surface slick. His yellow eyes are focused on my pussy, and he guides himself toward it with his mouth ajar, slipping between my lower lips.

Oh, fuck. I can't help the thought as that wide crown burrows its way inside me, soft and yet insistent. I'm just as needy for him as I am afraid that he might split me in half. My body struggles to accommodate him as he shoves himself in farther, that head asking me to open for it.

The more he stretches me, the greater the billow of pleasure spiraling up through my whole body. Somehow it's as wonderful as it is uncomfortable, delightful and delicious while I struggle to take it.

Shh, Graz murmurs, halting his progress. I realize I've been letting out little mewls. He looks down at me, his eyes soft as his thumb glances over my lip. *Let it settle.*

The sureness in his voice brings me down, and I let my head fall back and my muscles release. More of that thick cock slips into me, and I focus on allowing it inside.

Graz moans as he sinks in, filling every part of me, completely stuffing me. All my edges are widening for him, my body giving to him with pleasure.

There we are, he says, stroking my thigh as he pulls his hips back, withdrawing nearly to leaving me. *You're doing so well.* His second thrust is deeper but easier, and I expel a heavy breath as he pauses there, letting me adjust to him. His gaze is intent on me, his teeth gritted as he holds himself back.

He's making sure I enjoy this, and the care he's taking with me fans the flames of a slowly-growing fire.

Again Graz cants his hips back, and again he delves into me, somehow managing to fit even more of himself there. I'm wordless, enthralled, my nails digging into his arms as he continues gripping his cock.

I'm not even halfway inside you, Graz says with awe. His hand falls away, and he leans over me as he plunges in once more. I don't know how that's possible when I've already taken so much, but somehow I'm able to give another inch.

A cry slips out of me, and the unbearable wonder of the stretch has a trail of unfamiliar sounds leaving my mouth. It burns as much as it tantalizes, and on his next thrust, Graz manages to fit even more. I'm shivering all over, not from the cold, but from the sheer ecstasy of him, even though it's only just begun.

He drops down onto his forearms, so his face is much closer to mine. I writhe and snap my hips up, desperate for more. What is this orc doing to me? My arms snake around his neck, pulling him in closer as I long to see into his eyes again. His brows are creased, as if he's thinking and feeling the same thing I am—that we're not just doing what we need to do.

No, something of his is winding up with something of mine, unfurling between us with dew-tipped petals. My fingers disappear into his wet hair, and I clutch him close as he gently rocks inside me, letting me soften to him.

When he leans his forehead against mine, I close my eyes, simply delighting in the sensation of his big body, his heavy arms, his hips clasped between my thighs.

You're magnificent, his thoughts whisper, as if stroking the soft underbelly of my mind. *Your cunt is perfect. Made for me. Just for me.*

Just for you, I say without thinking about it, the words spilling out of me easily. *All for you.*

CHAPTER 11

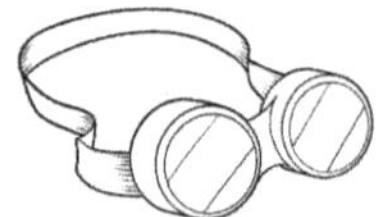

GRAZ

If I could, I would devour her so no other eyes ever get to see what I have.

This has taken on a new form, this heat between us, and I'm gentler with her than I ever intended to be. I can tell her little body—while it wants me as much as I want it—needs careful attention to make this pleasurable.

And I will make sure it's more than simply "pleasurable."

There is no sound at all like Vienne's high-pitched cries each time I test her depths, getting a sense of what she likes. I've never been tuned in to another being this way, as if I can feel what she feels in my bones, each stroke of my cock inside her red, swollen pussy ricocheting between us.

When her head falls back again, I can't help licking her exposed throat, drinking up the taste of her sweat. Her back arches, bringing her flush with my chest, and her arms draw me in even closer.

Fucking has always been something I did to expend energy,

to satisfy my instinct and move on. But this is a completely different act, as if at any moment, our bodies are going to envelop one another and turn us into a single writhing organism. I'm inside her and around her and a part of her, as if we were always meant to fit together.

When Vienne opens her eyes again, they spear me through the chest. That sensation constricts into a powerful tightness, one that can only be quenched by kissing her again and again. Fiercely I play with her tongue and lips, plundering them as thoroughly as I am her marvelous cunt.

Graz, please, I— Her thoughts are a jumble. *Please, don't stop.*

Never. I reel my hips back slowly, teasing her in circles before I dive into her again, managing to fit even more of myself in her small channel. I'm holding on tightly to my control, trying to claim as much of it as I can until she's perfectly ready for me.

She cries out again, her legs tightening around my hips, her heels digging into me as she begs for more. I want to see her, all of her, so I sit back and gaze down at her while I make her mine.

Mine. What a powerful word, and one that I know in my bones. Maybe she doesn't know it yet, but it's the truth. Now that I've tasted her, I could never forget it.

I don't know how all of this ends, but after this moment, I am sure of that single thing. Vienne is mine.

Armed with this newfound knowledge, I brace myself on the stone pedestal and pick up my pace, fucking her harder, reveling in the grip of her perfect body. When she clenches so tight around me I think I can't move, all sound ceases coming out of her. I can feel her pleasure ratcheting up as if it's in my own body, and around us...

The floor begins to glow. I'd be more alarmed by it if I

weren't being sucked into my little human, my eyes rolling back in my head as she squeezes so tightly I might just unspool. She's shaking all over with her final pleasure as I yank myself out and then slam into her again. Her voiceless scream gains sound, filling up the entire cavern around us. My very balls tighten, drawing up as my cock swells, and I groan a heavy, hot groan because I can't hold it back any longer.

Beneath us, the stone growls and shifts, and I feel us moving. But I'm helpless to do anything else but spill into her pulsing sheath. I roar as I pump inside her again, releasing it all as the purple light swells up higher and brighter around us. I am both invincible and horrifically vulnerable, reveling in the sweet milking of Vienne's flawless cunt while also knowing I have given up something invaluable to her, something I can never get back.

I hope I don't regret it.

When my fog clears, I realize that we've risen. Far below is a pool of glowing purple liquid, and I blink a few times to figure out what I'm seeing.

Magic, I whisper.

Definitely, Vienne says with satisfaction in her voice. *Wow. Didn't think you had that in you, orc.*

No, no. Look. I squint as I slowly withdraw from her, my cock dripping with both of us. I urge her forward on the pedestal carefully, so she doesn't topple off the side.

Oh. Holy shit. Vienne falls perfectly still when she peers over it. *There's so... much.*

We found it. Whatever is hidden here in this cave, we've opened it.

But first... I lie down on my side, too drained to be as elated as I'd thought I'd be when we discovered the secret. I feel like all the energy was sucked out of me and replaced with this heady bliss, and now all I want is to keep fucking my woman, over and over again. Vienne squeaks as I roll her up into my arms, feeling more certain of the truth with each passing second.

I've found my only, my everything.

My mate.

But I carefully keep my thoughts closed off from Vienne. I don't know what she, a human, would think of such a declaration. Humans don't have mates, and she's only just learned of the concept. Voicing this desire would be idiotic. I don't need to frighten her. No, I want her to choose me, to realize what I've realized, to understand the fact that we are now tied together for the rest of time. The idea of building a life, making whelps—that is for a very different moment.

At long last, I sit up and venture to the edge of the pedestal, where the pool of magic far down below us still glows. I help a naked Vienne up to her feet, and before we can step down, I pull her to me and kiss her fiercely. She's reeling when I release her, then I cautiously make my way to the edge of the platform. I lower myself down slowly, but Vienne simply hops off of it without a second look, plunging the six feet to the ground.

Oof. Hard landing. She rubs her feet as I finally drop to the floor beside her.

I'm going to worry a lot about this human, I can already tell.

We stand side by side and stare down past our feet at the gap that's now appeared between the platform and the floor. It's big enough to slide through, but who knows how far down it goes?

Don't worry, Vienne says, flapping a hand at me as if she can read my mind. *We can always use the magic to get back out again.*

It's flippant, but she's right. We have to investigate what's down there after we've come this far—and done this much.

What is this place, and why is it here? Who were all those humans and trollkin we saw in our vision?

Let me help you down this time, though, I tell her.

Vienne smirks, then navigates to the edge. I hold her hands tightly in mine as she slides off, into the darkness, and she's much lighter than I expected. I could throw her over my shoulder if I had to.

Something tells me that's a distinct possibility in the future.

There's a floor down here, she says, excited. *I can't tell how far down it is, but it's probably fine if you let me go.*

'Probably fine'?! I don't know if I like how callously Vienne regards her own life.

Instead of me releasing her, she slips her fingers through mine and drops.

Vienne!

I'm alright. I can almost hear the wink in her voice. *Come on down.*

I'm not nearly so thoughtless with my own limbs, so I navigate over the edge and down into the darkness cautiously, hanging as low as I can with one hand until the tips of my toes brush the floor.

See? she says brightly. *It's not so bad.*

With a grunt of annoyance, I let go and drop the rest of the way down. The purple glow of magic is so bright here it's nearly blinding, but when I turn away, my eyes are able to adjust to the dark.

Vienne stands silhouetted against more carvings, the deep channels filled with magic. These are very different designs, though. I come to stand beside her as we take in the walls around us.

There are figures everywhere, but they all lead up a mountain toward two individuals—one human and one trollkin, their hands raised into the air as one. Opposite them is what appears to be a massive, curling worm.

I trace over the worm's outline with my fingers.

The tunnels, Vienne says in wonder. *That's one of the ancient worms, who made all those tunnels in the desert.*

I turn to her, arching a brow. *In the desert?*

I found some in the Hazrain with the rest of the History Corps. Ancient tunnels carved by the worms, which humans or trollkin then later occupied. I think that's what this is.

I know of what she's talking about. I've seen drawings of the massive skeletons out in the desert.

I thought the worms all went extinct?

Vienne shrugs. A beam is erupting from the couple's joined hands, streaking out toward the worm like a blast of flame. I have no idea what it means, but it looks like the memory of a great battle fought once upon a time.

Is that magic, do you think? Vienne asks. *Coming out of her hands?*

Maybe. What makes you think so?

Her jaw tightens. *Just seems powerful, that's all.*

You're right about that. I inhale sharply, remembering just how destructive magic can be. *One of the other sites I went to... the whole damned place blew up.*

Her eyes get big. *What?*

In Morgenzan. I believe there was magic there, too. I remember arriving in the middle of a huge conflict, the very earth shaking with the fury of it. The Grand Chieftain was mining the mountain, but by the time I got there, it was all up in flames.

Vienne turns back to the pool, regarding it with suspicion. *I thought so.*

I cock my head. *You thought what?*

I knew this stuff was bad news. She leans down to scoop some up into her palm, regarding it with suspicion. *We can't let anyone else get their hands on this.*

I agree wholeheartedly with that. *I don't think that will happen. And it's not inherently nefarious.* I scoop some up myself. *It's a tool like any other.*

And I know just what I need to use it for right now.

I stand and tilt my hand, feeding the magic my desire before letting the droplets spill out onto the floor. Slowly, the purple ooze shifts and grows, sprouting up from the ground to form the metal shape of a great big tub. Vienne gets to her feet, eyes wide as the tub fills with water, and soon steam is rising from the surface.

Vienne's mouth broadens as she sees what I've created for her. *Is that a bath?* she asks in a voice too breathless to hope.

A warm bath. I grab her by the hips and lift her up, then settle her down in the hot water.

Ooh, hot, hot! She wriggles as I get into the tub with her, adjusting our legs so now she's resting on top of mine, her little feet sitting to either side of my waist. The water lifts Vienne's breasts in an appealing manner, and in turn, the head of my cock floats to the surface.

All right, she hedges, sinking lower into the water to submerge herself. *This isn't bad, I have to admit.*

I grin, knowing exactly what it would take to convince her. She leans back against the opposite wall of the tub, resting her head there and closing her eyes. While she relaxes, I take one of her teeny, adorable feet in my hands, first admiring her five little toes, then rubbing my thumb down the sole.

"Ooh," Vienne hums out loud. *That's good.*

I continue my work on her left foot, until she's little more than a human body full of jelly, then I switch to her right foot. I make my way up her thighs, leaning forward so I can rub her muscles and touch even more of her skin. I want her even closer, so close I could simply eat her.

What a bizarre sensation. I've never experienced such a deep affection for someone, especially someone I barely know. But I just want to pull her into the ring of my arms and bind our bodies together, so she can never leave me.

Finally, when I'm done with both her thighs and the water has gone tepid, we rise out of the bath. Not long after, the tub itself vanishes.

So strange, Vienne says, eyeballing where it used to be. While she's standing there, wet and skeptical, I scoop out some more magic from the pool.

I know what else I want to do with it, what other things I can create. Then, perhaps, I can convince her of what I know to be true.

<h1 style="text-align:center">Chapter 12</h1>

Vienne

Graz gives me a wicked, boyish grin as he tips his hand, letting another handful of purple, glowing magic to slide out of his palm. Before it even hits the floor, it starts glowing brighter, changing shape and spreading wider and wider. It grows up from the ground, turning into what appears to be... a four-poster bed?

As the purple glow fades, I'm sure that's what he's made. It's covered in thick blankets and furs, with piles of pillows all over it like it belongs to some king or noble.

I stare, blinking like a moron. A big, soft, cozy bed, right here in the middle of this cold, stone cavern?

Yes, please.

I dive for the bed, grabbing a pillow as I roll over to dry myself off on the soft furs. Graz chuckles as he sits down beside me, taking another fur for himself, while I wriggle under the blankets.

Wow, I say, awed. *You know the meaning of luxury.*

He shoots me a wide grin as he pulls the blankets aside and slides in next to me, whirling me up in his arms. Then he curls his hand under my ass, squeezing it as he watches my thoughts pass over my face. Even though we just fucked, my body awakens at his mere touch.

He cradles my breast in his other hand, flicking one finger over my nipple in a way that feels practiced, familiar. He moves farther down to the space between my thighs, and one finger glides along the outside of my pussy. I'm already warm and swelling up quickly for him, just anticipating what he's going to do next.

Then Graz's finger sinks into me, and I moan. Of their own accord, my hands find their way down between us to where his cock is already hard for me, jutting up between our bellies. I stroke it gently, and his eyelids fall to half-mast. His hips push into my hands as I run my palm over his cockhead, where he's already dripping for me from the tip.

We touch one other that way for what feels like a small eternity, measuring each other's reactions, finding what we like best. Maybe this isn't necessary, but what do I have against a little recreation?

Graz teases my clit, strumming it like an expert player before he slips two fingers inside me. There he strokes, testing all the different spots available to him until I'm gasping and twitching, grinding myself against his hand.

You like that? he asks, pinching my nipple as his fingers work harder, fucking into me and then retreating to tantalize my bud again. In turn, I increase the pressure of my hand around his cock, squeezing with every pump.

Not enough. My thoughts come out as pathetic whimpers.

A wicked smile crosses my orc's face, and I love how it's lopsided, so his left tusk rises higher than his right.

There's still so much of me inside you, Graz croons, and there's an erotic sound as he starts to thrust those fingers in and out of me faster. *I'll fit just right in here.*

My whole body alights at this suggestion. That's exactly what I need.

Damn. I'm already obsessed with this orc.

He tilts up my chin so I'm forced to look into his unfamiliar eyes, with the yellow sclera and amber iris. Then he kisses me, hard.

This time, I lie with my back to Graz's front as he spreads the cheeks of my ass and lifts my thigh to wedge himself between them. There's no pedestal underneath us this time, no vision guiding us to do what we have to do.

No, my body is begging now for what it wants, and that's him. What's the harm in indulging, while we're here?

Graz spreads the swollen, puffy lips of my sex and guides that massive cock inside me. I'm so slick, so stretched already, that he fits in smoothly. He pushes through until he's seated as far inside me as he can be, and a string of nonsense escapes my lips.

It's as if we've reunited and fit back into the place we belong. I fall into him, letting him consume me from the inside out.

GRAZ

I could fuck Vienne forever.

Her body gleefully swallows me up, encasing me in her pristine warmth. I shut my eyes to hold back my finish, because I'm already so close with just one stroke. How does she do this to me? I can jerk off for an hour, but one taste of her and I'm at the precipice.

I shove it down, breathing hard to bring myself back to center before I shunt my hips back, then slide into her again. This time, I push even deeper, opening my eyes so I can take in the sight of my cock spreading her red, swollen cunt wide. How this little human can take me is a wondrous mystery, and I'll relish every moment of it.

While I'm inside her, I sneak a hand underneath her, soaking my fingers in our fluids and using it to graze over her clit. Vienne lets out a sound that's close to a squeal, and her entire channel tightens perilously around me.

I grit my teeth as I nearly withdraw, then sink back into her again, pushing through it while I tease her.

"Ah!" She reaches back to grip any part of me she can. I love how she has to be touching at all times, as fully as possible. *More, please!* she calls out frantically.

Whatever she requires, I will provide—whether it's food, drink, or my cock. I lean back to get a better angle, holding her thigh up to spread her open for me, and plunge into her tiny cunt again and again.

Vienne balls up the blanket and bites down, moaning into it as I thrust harder, tormenting her clit faster. I plan to make her come around me until I've wrung every last droplet of pleasure out of her, until she has no choice but to stay with me.

You feel perfect, I tell her as I sink deep, then yank myself out again, her cries growing in volume. She's helpless, gripping the blankets, bucking back into me with every pump of my hips. *Your cunt is sublime. I can't get enough. I'm going to fuck it full, until you're covered in me.*

I didn't think I was a dirty talker, but I can't seem to stop. I need her to know how amazing she feels around me, how beautiful she is, how much I need her.

How much I don't know if I can live without her.

I know it's foolish. I gave Lo'zar an earful for doing exactly what I'm doing, but I can't help myself. It's taken over my mind how much I want to fuck my seed as deeply into her as possible, and this thought makes me thrust even faster, my breaths coming hot and heavy.

When Vienne clamps down tight around me, I know I've won. She sobs out her bliss as I slam into her once more, and my own pleasure erupts. I groan as my climax is practically ripped from me, and my cock pulses as I fill her, luxuriating in her with one more wet, squelching stroke.

Even after I unleash, I stay hard. She's trembling all over as I push all my spend back into her.

More? Vienne says, then gasps aloud as I squeeze as much of myself into her tightened cunt as I can. She shivers around me, clearly still aroused as my seed spills out of her.

Always more.

I continue wringing the bliss from her little body, each wet stroke making her scream words I can't understand, until finally, we're both spent. In a wholly different position from when we started, Vienne lets out a whine, her face buried in my chest as I work my cock free of her tiny, swollen sex.

I think I'm going to hurt tomorrow.

I cup her dripping pussy in my hand to soothe it. *Guess I'll just have to lick it until it feels better, then.*

She shivers at my words, and I feel quite smug knowing she's just as attracted to me as I am to her. Vienne may not understand the bond, but I'm sure that it's settling in with her the same way. It's just a matter of time.

I'm hoping that she'll accept what I'm going to offer her, knowing there's a good chance she won't. I can't take a second with her for granted if she's only going to walk out of my life at the end of this.

Vienne

By the time Graz is done with me, I'm drenched in him as he promised, my thighs sticky and wet. We've fucked in just about every position imaginable on our new magical bed, and I don't know how he's managed to keep it up so long.

I don't think I can orgasm even once more as I collapse, burying my face in one of the many soft pillows. Graz slings one leg over my hip, as if we've done this a million times before, and loops his arms around me.

I could simply fall asleep this way, but I don't want the bed to vanish while I'm passed out on it. It's wonderful and marvelous what we can do with magic. That Graz has summoned every one of his wishes out of thin air, though, also makes me afraid.

It is far too much power for any mortal individual to wield. Especially the wrong one. Mom was absolutely right—if the King or the Grand Chieftain got their hands on this, they could do untold damage.

After a time, Graz rises from the bed and summons us a whole banquet of food. I'm sure the food won't last inside my belly after I've eaten it, but that doesn't stop me from devouring every piece of honey-basted pork I can. This will be my final opportunity to enjoy this, anyway.

I wipe my chin. *I can't believe this was just waiting here for the last... who knows how long?* Are we really the first to have seen this, to have witnessed this, since ancient times?

Graz snickers. *Well, given the requirements for getting inside, I can't say I'm surprised.* He thoughtfully strokes my shoulder.

I didn't mind having some really amazing sex, I joke. *Who taught you all that?*

He blinks. *Nobody? It's never been like that before.*

Something about those words makes me feel light and airy. So only I turn him on like this?

It's never been like that for me before, either, I have to admit.

But it wasn't just us doing... you know. That opened the pedestal and revealed what's inside. Graz clears his throat, even though he's speaking in his mind.

I lift my head. *Then what did?*

It's the kind *of sex we had.* He reaches under my chin and tips it up so I have to look into his eyes.

What kind is that?

He's quiet for a long time, almost too long. Then he says, *The kind that mates have.*

I stare at him. There's no way.

Graz said that word before. Explained it to me in the simplest terms. But whatever this *mate* thing is, it's not me. I barely know this orc, and he's certainly not my "mate." There can't be anything between us, not beyond this moment. We did what we had to do to access this secret, that's all. And some bonuses.

I pull away from him, frowning. *You have it all wrong,* I say firmly. *I'm not your mate.*

We just fucked a few times. It might have been incredible —mind blowing and life changing, honestly—but it's still just that: a good fuck. It doesn't mean anything more.

I hate the look Graz gets on his face like he already knew I'd say that.

You're human, he says, leaning on one elbow, still stroking my side. *I don't know if humans feel it the same way. But I know right here.* He rubs his chest. *It's true.*

Well, that's just it, isn't it? I'm human, he's not. Maybe he thinks there's something between us because of who he is, because he's trollkin, but that doesn't mean *matehood* binds me the same way.

I want to climb off this bed, slide my clothes back on and put some distance between us again, but then Graz wraps his arm around me and brings me in close. He neatly tucks my head under his chin and smooths one big, four-fingered hand down my back, which has the perplexing effect of calming me.

I know it's probably strange to you, he says in a quieter voice that somehow, feels closer to my own mind than before. *It's strange to me, too. I always knew the mate bond existed, but not what it felt like.*

My curiosity piques. I understand very little about trollkin culture. *What does it feel like?*

Graz strokes my hair with a tenderness no one's ever shown me. *Like going home—to a home I never knew I had.* Now he's tracing my cheek with his index finger and studying me like an artifact. *Finding peace in someone else's hands, knowing all you want is to rest your head beside theirs.*

I suppose that right here, right now, with Graz's big arm slung around me and his soft palm on my face, it's as if my spirit has finally found its match. But it might just be a post-coital glow.

You feel that way? I ask. *Really?*

Graz searches my eyes, his brow creasing as if what he has to say is going to frighten me away.

Seems crazy. He sighs and lays his head down, coasting his hand down my side to my hip. *But I feel like I've known you my whole life.*

Maybe I do understand it. Ever since my father died, Mom and I have both felt like we lost a connection to where we came from, to the thing that rooted us to the earth. It had seemed impossible at the time that someone who was so important to me, so closely bound to my soul, had simply vanished.

And yet here, right now, it feels like some of the loneliness has passed. Like maybe I've found something that could help me put down roots again, and make sense of the chaotic world we live in.

I find myself snuggling in closer, and Graz hums as he holds me tight. I don't know if he's right about this bond between us, but perhaps a part of me hopes that he is.

CHAPTER 13

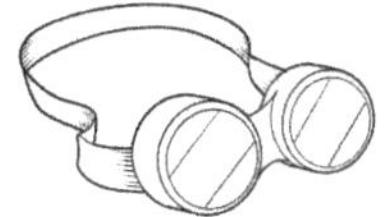

GRAZ

I've cut open my own heart and revealed it to her, and now it's a matter of what she'll do with it. Will she accept me, and decide she feels the same way? As she falls asleep in my arms, I don't think I can possibly let her go.

We awake some time later, and my cock is rock hard pressed against her ass. Still, I manage to slip away, returning to the magic pool to summon us some more food. I bring a big platter of roast beef and sweet potatoes to the bed, and naked, we both eat as much as we can. Vienne lifts a cherry and puts it between my lips, then leans up to kiss me, biting off half of it as she does.

She is a sensual and romantic woman, I think. And perfect for me. But what comes next? What comes after this?

Maybe we should leave, Vienne suggests after we've cleaned up the food, and the bed has vanished. I still want to fuck her again, but I think that will occupy a good part of my mind for the rest of time.

Leave and go where? I ask. I still haven't gotten my answer about how she feels, though I've bared my heart to her.

Vienne's lips screw up. *Well, get out of this cold cave, for starters. And then...* She offers me a small smile. *Figure out what comes next? I left everything behind to come here. I abandoned the King's History Corps.*

That sounds like it was a big deal for you.

She sighs. *My life's work. But... this was bigger than that. And now I have nothing to go back to.*

I nod in understanding. She has her mother, but without her work, there isn't much holding her down. Unfortunately, this world—as I've learned from seeing Lo'zar and Rimi struggle—isn't kind to a match like ours.

Perhaps we should go to a neutral city. I'm perfectly happy abandoning my shop in Kalishagg if it means I could be with Vienne for the long haul. I can't imagine giving her up now. *We might be safe there.*

She studies me as she sits on the edge of the pool. I join her there, slipping an arm around her waist to show her I plan to stay with her.

What about your life? she asks, tilting her head. *You would just give that up for me?*

Of course. I'd give up anything for you. I haven't known her long, but I know this truth deep down. Anywhere my mate goes, I'll go with her.

Vienne's expression falters, as if these aren't the words she expected to hear.

Oh. She looks down at her lap, her expression puzzled. *Why do I feel like I'd do the same for you?*

I grin. So I'm not the only one feeling it. Our life together plays in front of my mind's eye—living in a neutral city together where we might be safe, filling her up with whelps, fucking every night and every morning again.

A hope I never could have possibly imagined blooms inside me. Perhaps I've found what Lo'zar found. I pull Vienne into my lap, burying my face in her hair to breathe in the perfect scent of her. I won't forget that smell for as long as I live.

That's the mate bond. I nuzzle her as I hold her close. How my best friend would laugh if he saw me now, after all the hassle I gave him.

Well then, Vienne says. *I suppose we had better go and figure it out.* She rises, then holds out a hand to me. I take it, dwarfing hers in mine. I'll never get tired of how cute and small she is.

Once more, I pull her against me and kiss her deeply, and she squeaks before she returns it. Then it's time to go and figure out what our life looks like from here.

When I've released her, we both dress, then Vienne kneels by the pool of glowing magic and scoops some out. She closes her eyes and spills it on the floor. Rather than dissipating, it slithers along the stone, until it starts to extend up into the air. Right in front of me, it forms a rather convincing wooden ladder.

She gestures with her chin. *You first.*

With a nod of agreement, I start to climb. I'm ready to get out of this cavern and see the light of day again.

Vienne

The moment Graz is out of sight, I crouch down, opening my water skin, and fill it from the glowing purple pool. Who knows when I'll need it—or what I'll need it for. Once I do what I came here to do, this will be all that's left.

Then I scoop some more magic into my hand and make my intention clear.

"Dissolve into nothing," I whisper to it, pouring it back into the stone basin that surrounds the base of the pedestal. "Become poison. Never let anyone else use what we've found here."

The droplet hits the surface, and instantly, it turns black.

I turn around and head for the ladder, then scurry my way up as fast as I can. When I reach the top and peer down, I see the black droplet has already begun to spread, infecting the rest of the pool.

Graz's eyes follow mine, and his brows shoot into his hair. *What's happening?*

Just go, I tell him, kneeling to pull up the ladder behind us. Then I snatch my pack up off the floor, and toss the other to Graz. After slinging it on, he grabs the ladder and carries it with us.

What did you do? he demands again, setting the ladder against the wall. It's just high enough that it will get us out of here.

I don't answer as I hop onto the bottom rung. Then, all around us, the very rock rumbles.

Stones start falling from the ceiling. The black is spreading through the cavern itself now, and I hurry my climb as Graz gets onto the ladder behind me.

Go fast! I bark at him, scrambling higher. The walls are rattling, bigger and bigger stones falling as the black magic works its way upward.

Fuck. I didn't think it would destroy the whole damned place.

Finally I reach the top, and grab onto the ledge to pull myself up. Graz isn't far behind me, but the ladder could go out from under him at any time.

Graz! I grab his outstretched hand and yank on him as hard as I can. The ladder gives way right as he hooks his other hand on the ledge, and I help him climb up onto it with me.

Then we meet the narrow stone hallway that led us in here in the first place. With the roof falling down, we need to get out—now.

Go! Go! I shove him forward and, without question, Graz obeys, sprinting into the darkness with his lamp held out. The roof is caving in, and a few small stones hit me in the head and shoulders as we run. I reel from the blows, but Graz reaches back and snatches up my hand in his before dragging me along behind him.

Finally, we emerge into the fresh air, bathed in morning sunlight. It's morning? I completely lost track of time in there.

The rumbling is still audible, even out here.

We can't stop, Graz says, panting. He pushes me toward the stairs leading down the cliffside, and I start running down them as fast as is safe. Now it's as if the entire mountain itself is crumbling.

What did you do in there? he yells again as I nearly slip on the steps.

I did what had to be done.

But I wonder if I made the right choice.

GRAZ

I don't know what she means, but I'm too busy trying to live to parse it out.

We make our way carefully down the steps, Vienne moving faster than I am, clearly more practiced with things like running down a staircase with no railing while the entire mountain comes apart next to you.

But what did she do back there? What could have caused this?

Then, the rock right under my feet cracks open.

Vienne picks up her pace, and I know we're playing with our lives as we both sprint down the stone stairs. The cracks are spreading, and this must be how Lo'zar felt, trying to escape that ruin with his and his mate's lives.

Not my favorite position to be in.

Finally, we're near the bottom when the tip of the cliffside completely falls off the top. The rock under my feet breaks apart, and I leap forward, clearing three more steps and nearly falling onto Vienne. Instead, I grab her around the waist and pull her down on top of me as I skid on my back to the ground, hoping to cushion her fall.

Fuck, that hurts.

We have to keep going, Vienne says, panicked. She crawls to her feet and then takes off running again, her pack bouncing on her back.

I follow quickly behind her. *Why? What are we running from?*

She glances at me over her shoulder as another terrible cracking sound fills the air. *I destroyed it.*

I slow down my run. *You what?* I pause, then turn around to look up at the mountainside behind us. Sure enough, the rock has turned black as onyx.

No. I can't believe what I'm seeing. *You didn't.*

Then Vienne's hand grabs mine. *Run, you idiot!*

Turning around, I take off after her as another huge chunk of rock tumbles to the ground, landing shockingly close to us—close enough that clods of dirt fly into the air and hit me in the face.

So we run, and run, until we're enveloped in the woods and

the mountain is far behind us. But my heart is blazing with fury. She's betrayed me.

We found something marvelous, something priceless down there, and my mate has obliterated it.

I was wrong about her.

<h1 style="text-align:center">CHAPTER 14</h1>

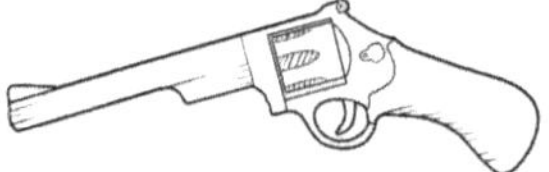

I know he's going to be angry with me, and now, as the entire mountain breaks apart behind us, I'm not so sure it was worth it.

But Mom is right. Despite the fun games we played, not everyone in the world is like Graz. Magic is too dangerous to exist, too dangerous to be trusted. If the powers that be discovered it, they would use it to destroy each other—and all of us would be caught in the middle.

When we've left the crumbling mountain far behind, I slow down to gasp for air. My legs and lungs both are burning, and Graz stumbles to rest against a nearby tree.

You did this? he asks, horror in his voice. He glares at me, panting.

I let out a deep sigh. *Yes. And it was the right thing to do. You know what could happen if what we found fell into the wrong hands.*

That doesn't mean you should have destroyed it! He smashes a fist against the tree. *We could have protected it. Made sure that no one else discovered it. We could have used it to make the world better!*

It's too dangerous, I say. *You know it. You know what would happen if someone powerful got their hands on it, what kind of damage they could do. They could destroy the world!*

When Graz levels his gaze on me, his eyes are aflame.

You should have asked me. We could have discussed it. But you just made the decision on your own! Now we can't find out what those carvings mean. What if it was important? He fists his hands in his wild hair. *I can't believe you!*

We saw it, I argue. *We witnessed it. Now it's buried where no one else will find it.*

But Graz says nothing as he stares at me, trembling with rage. He sucks in a deep breath, adjusts his pack on his back, and with one final, scathing glare, he turns around and strides off.

Where are you going? I ask, perplexed. I thought that after everything he said about being *mates,* we would go searching for the last marker on the map together. We could bury the last evidence of magic that exists, and make sure no one else ever gets their hands on it.

Away. Far, far away from you. He marches on. *I can't even stand to look at you.*

I stare at his retreating back as he leaves me, and my heart beats faster.

What was all that back in the cavern? I didn't think this was possible after everything he said—that he would just turn around and walk away.

You're leaving? I ask, though it's obvious that's what he intends. He's going to abandon me.

Graz doesn't answer. My chest constricts, tightening around my lungs as he walks on without a second thought.

The hurt from knowing what we did back in that cavern, how he looked into my eyes and kissed me like I was his everything, all those sweet words he told me... it twists and shifts into anger.

I knew it, I yell after him. *I knew you were lying. It was just your dick talking when you said all that mate bullshit to me, wasn't it?*

This is all I need to be sure that he made it up. When Graz doesn't answer, my face heats.

Fine! Go! I don't give a fuck what happens to you! I clench my hands into fists as an unfamiliar sensation bites at the backs of my eyes.

I won't fucking cry over an orc. I won't.

And still, Graz says nothing as he disappears into the trees.

GRAZ

I must have been wrong back there in the cavern about who she is to me.

We don't know each other. This shows exactly how little I understand this human woman—that she would extinguish what meager light we have with which to peer into the past. That she would destroy something ancient and precious, something we've barely begun to understand.

I thought we were kindred spirits, drawn by the secrets of the past, intent on discovering the truth. But we have nothing in common. I have curiosity, while she is destruction.

My guts ache and my heart pulls like a taut rope as the distance between us grows. But fate was wrong this time. Vienne isn't mine—she is a curse. That she would do this behind my back, that she'd betray me in such a profound way... it's a gift wrapped in poison.

I try to block out her angry thoughts as I leave her there. If she thinks I am a traitor, then she knows how I feel.

I could never be mated to someone so callous and foolish.

You trollkin are all the same, she says, still so close and present in my thoughts even though she's a long way behind me. *Deceitful and cruel. I knew I was right not to trust you with it.*

I still don't answer. She can think what she likes about me. I'm never going to see her again anyway.

Vienne continues berating me as I walk, until the volume of her thoughts begins to fade. Soon, I'm trudging alone through the forest, heading uphill as I make my way back to the path that brought me here.

Alone. That's always how it's been, and always how it will be. I don't need her.

But my whole body aches as I go.

When I reach the closest town after a few days of hard walking, I sit down at the bar in the local tavern, ready to drink myself into a stupor. Once I've got a beer in front of me, I pull out my map. If Vienne has the same information I do, she could already be headed to the fourth marker. It's far up in human territory to the east.

I need to get there before she does.

I'm halfway through my beer when one very large troll and one very large orcess sit down to either side of me. The orcess, whose hulking body blocks out the light, is familiar—I think she's one of Gusak's goons.

Oh.

"The boss wants a word with you," the troll says close to

my ear as the orcess grabs my beer and slugs it back. "We've been waiting a while for you to show up."

Why would Gusak send them after me? Has he been keeping tabs on me?

Now I understand. He didn't believe me for a moment last time we spoke, and he suspected I was up to more than I shared—so he sent these two along to tail me. They must have lost me here in town, and waited for me to return.

"Fine," I say with a sigh, sliding a few coins across the bar to cover my beer and the food I'd ordered, but probably won't get to eat now. "You want me to come now, I presume?"

The troll nods. "Now."

When we step out into the afternoon, the sun is shining hot and oppressive.

"Did you have something to do with that mountain collapsing?" the orcess asks, surveying the skyline. "It was the talk of the town. We felt it all the way here."

Great. I'm not going to be able to hide magic from Gusak any longer after they witnessed that.

"Yeah." I shake my head. "A mistake I'll never be able to take back."

The troll whistles. "Impressive! You took down a whole mountain? How much dynamite did you use?"

I don't answer.

Once the orc and the troll gather up three horses, we're on our way. Thankfully they don't tie me up, but it's obvious I have nowhere to go or they'll certainly come after me. And I have low hopes for what I'll face when we return to Kalishagg.

Every step away from those mountains feels like I'm leaving something behind I'll never get back.

Vienne

When Graz doesn't turn around after more than an hour, I finally stop yelling after him. It won't do any good. He's decided.

He threw me away. As angry as I am, I'm not surprised, either. What happened was nothing. Any meaning I read into it is just that—something I made up, something I wanted to believe in because nobody has ever wanted me just for *me*.

Everything Graz said was a lie.

This rejection shouldn't hurt as much as it does, though. It shouldn't feel like a sharp cut into my chest, a blade burying itself deep and then twisting until I feel like I'm choking on my own blood.

I skate my hand over the handle of my pistol. Maybe I should've shot him. Maybe that very first time we met, I should've done the right thing and ended him.

Well, I won't mess up a second time.

I'm even more certain in my mission now. Magic is a danger. I can't let that orc, or any of his kind, get their hands on it—which means I have to beat him to the last marker on the map. I'll have to pass through Culberra on my way, but then I can tell Mom what I've done.

There will be some parts I leave out of that story.

It takes eons to get back to the little human town far to the south where the train passes through, and I have to use some of my magic along the way just to feed myself. The days drag on as I hike, recounting every last thing that happened in that cavern, my fury growing and then abating whenever I think of what Graz and I did together.

By the time I reach my destination, all my anger has faded into a resigned melancholy. I'm aching all over, my legs exhausted from how hard I pushed them the last few days, my body tired to the core.

It feels even deeper than that, but I try not to think about it. It's easier if I gloss over everything that transpired in that cave and pretend it never happened.

I sleep most of the train ride back to Culberra, but in my dreams, Graz looks into my eyes, and I can't tear myself away from looking back.

CHAPTER 15

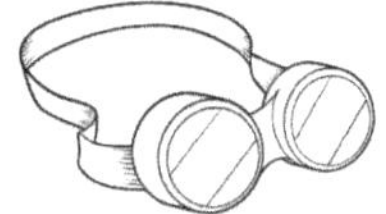

GRAZ

The troll, the orcess and I don't speak much as we ride for the port, where the same boat I arrived on is waiting to take us back to the city. But I do manage to pry an explanation out of the troll, Kal'zan.

Gusak sent his minions to tail me the moment I left Kalishagg, suspecting I'd lied to him. At least they didn't get their hands on Vienne. There's one that small sliver of light in everything that's happened. I despise her, and hate viciously what she's done, but when I picture her small, tanned face and big blue eyes, I'm overwhelmed by how much I miss her. How I would have loved to stay in that cavern forever, buried in her exquisite cunt, before she ruined everything.

Despite that, I have to keep Gusak away from her.

This is all really the worst possible outcome. I've lost my mate, I've lost the pool of magic, and I've lost my freedom. Everything is gone in a blink, and I had no choice in the matter.

I have very little will left by the time we reach Kalishagg. I don't need to be tied up to follow my two captors back to my shop, then down the elevator to the hideout. Kugara gives me a pitying look as we pass her.

I wonder if this is her fault, too. Perhaps she cracked and told Gusak about the map.

We descend the steps, the way lit by torches reflecting off the multicolored crystals that shoot out from every surface. Usually I see this place as home, but now it might be my tomb if Gusak thinks I've betrayed him.

At last we reach Gusak's level, and I'm led to his personal rooms. The troll and the orcess deposit me on a chair, tying my arms down to it, then stand at either doorway until Gusak joins us.

He does not look as angry as I'd expected when he slips into the room then shuts the door firmly behind him. In fact, there's a hint of a smile pulling at his lip as he strides in. And, oddly, there are a pair of glasses perched atop his nose, which I've never seen before.

The boss doesn't wear glasses, does he?

"Ah, my errant mechanic." He unties the cloak over his shoulders and lays it over the back of a chair before sitting down across from me. "Going off on his little adventures."

I screw up my lips. How much does he know? How deep is the shit I'm in? I swallow roughly.

"What did you find out?" the boss says, leaning forward and propping his elbows on his knees. "I know you're investigating some map that Kugara found—and erroneously gave to you instead of giving it to me."

Fuck. She told him, just like I thought. Death could very well be in the cards for me now.

At least he hasn't come across the bag of magic I've hidden among my old parts. But there's no point in lying to Gusak about what I found, not after he already suspects me. He'll see right through it, and then my punishment will be even greater.

"I'm sorry," I begin, but Gusak waves a hand at me dismissively.

"You know I detest a liar in my ranks, bookworm."

I shrivel in my seat. I remember how furious he was when Lo'zar double-crossed him by stealing the human woman, Rimi. Gusak was ready to kill anyone who was involved, and I barely scraped by. If he finds out I helped them, he might tear my limbs off one by one while I'm still alive to serve as a warning to others.

Then what would happen to Vienne? Have we bonded deeply enough that it would take her life, too?

"But I'm giving you a slim, slim pass this time," Gusak continues. "Because I am very interested in what you've discovered—and what it means for the clan."

"What I've discovered...?" I wonder if he knows just how much I've hidden from him.

Gusak snickers. "Agna told me about your suspicious little pendant. And that whole mountain you brought down with you." He stoops and fishes in my shirt for the pendant, then withdraws it. "I know you're after something, something you've been keeping secret, and I wonder why."

I shudder. "Because it's dangerous. It could do an incredible amount of damage in the wrong hands, as you saw."

Gusak arches a brow as he studies the glowing vial. "And you don't trust me with it, I assume."

I bite my lip, unsure of how to answer. I only managed to scrape by the skin of my teeth when Gusak questioned me about Lo'zar escaping onto a ship with his stolen human.

"You're right, I don't," I say at last. "But it's not about you!" I add hastily. "I... I don't trust anyone not to do something terrible with it."

"Hmm." Gusak studies me. "But you are the exception?"

I suppose I have used magic for my own selfish ends. Multiple times. I almost blush remembering it.

"So what's inside the necklace?" Gusak prompts when I don't answer. "Do I have to dangle you over the alligator pit?"

I shudder. He'll do whatever he has to do to get the truth out of me, and I know that if he tried to tear off my fingernails or break my limbs, I wouldn't last.

Swallowing hard, I close my eyes as I say the words. "It's magic."

The room is silent, and when I finally dare to look up at Gusak again, his face is colored with genuine surprise.

"Magic? Real magic? The kind in old fairy tales?"

I bite my lip and nod. Perhaps I am a mite grateful that Vienne destroyed that pool of magic we found, because that's one less chance for Gusak to retrace my steps and uncover it for himself.

The boss hums and scratches his chin. "Magic. I'd say you're trying to pull the wool over my eyes, but that would be stupid of you, wouldn't it? And you're not stupid, bookworm."

"I try not to be."

The boss drops forward so we're closer to eye level. "What else can it do?" he asks.

I lick my lips, wishing I didn't have to answer this. But if I get dropped into a pit full of alligators, who knows what would happen to Vienne?

"It can do anything you want." I feel sick as I say it, as I reveal this dangerous information to an orc like Gusak. "I still haven't found a limit, though I am suspicious of trying certain things. I once summoned Izzy from a great distance, and he hasn't been the same since." My lizard is still a little rattled by it, acting confused and wandering into objects in his way—but he's getting better. "And it has a time limit. What you create with it doesn't last forever."

"I understand. You think you are doing the world a service by keeping it secret."

Uncertainly, I nod.

"You would even lie to me," Gusak goes on, "believing it's the right thing to do, and put yourself at extreme risk."

My anxiety is thrumming, my blood rushing too fast as I contemplate my punishment.

"Who else knows about this?" Gusak asks me.

I know how my boss feels about humans. He locked one in a cage and sold her like an exotic animal. If I tell him about Vienne, who knows what he'll do to me?

"Don't lie," Gusak warns. "You're terrible at hiding it, and you need all your fingers if you want to keep turning wrenches."

I shut my eyes. I hope Vienne got far away. I hope she's hidden deep in human territory again, where she's safe.

"The only other one who knows is... a human." I don't know what she plans to do with the magic she gathered in her water skin, but it's not outside the realm of possibility that she'll do exactly what I feared and hand it over to the human king. "She was with me. She's seen what it can do."

Gusak's eyes narrow as he leans farther forward. "You shared this secret with a human, but not with me?"

"Nothing like that. She discovered it on her own. And... she destroyed it. One of the locations we found, anyway."

It looks like I've actually taken my boss by surprise. "She's the one who blew up the mountain?"

Great. I'm going to have to reveal much more than I'd hoped if I want to keep all my body parts attached to me.

"It's a long story."

VIENNE

The city is bustling, as always, but this time I'm separate from them, no longer a part of the mass of swirling bodies. I've seen the dark insides of the world, and I've done things I can never take back.

I'll never be able to undo what Graz and I discovered in that cavern, or what I did after it.

The first thing I do is wander back to my own apartment, then fall face-first onto my bed. It feels like I don't get back up for eons. I know I need to move quickly to get to the last location, but I would almost rather that the earth swallow me up.

After bathing, eating, sleeping, and wallowing for a while longer, I know what I have to do.

I wander deep into the city, toward the archive. The door is locked, as always, and I have to wait quite a while for Mom to come and answer it.

She squints in the sunlight, then urges me to enter.

"What did you find?" she asks, before anything else. It's easy to see where I get it from.

"I did it." I exhale a breath I've been holding for the last two weeks of traveling. "We found—I mean, *I* found the ruin in the Stoneteeth. Right where you thought it would be."

She doesn't appear surprised by this. "What did you do with it?"

"The magic? I took some and destroyed the rest."

"Ah." Mom nods in understanding. "Good."

She gives me an approving smile, like that's another matter resolved. It helps that she agrees with my decision, but I still feel a sinking sensation in my belly when I think about turning all that magic black.

"The whole mountain came down with it, though."

Mom squints at me. "Explain."

When we've settled at her desk, I tell her about finding the cavern, leaving out that Graz met me there and pretending I did it alone. I wish I'd drawn the carvings we found to show it to her, but I do my best to describe it, scribbling out what I remember onto a piece of paper.

"Hmm." She rises from her chair and, without a word, heads down into one of the darkened shelves. A few minutes later, she returns with a book I've seen before—back when I was a little girl.

"What's that?"

Returning to her chair, she opens the book to one of the many notes stuck inside the pages.

"A story. A legend. A children's tale." She flips to an illustration, and sets it out in front of me.

It's a simple watercolor painting of a human woman with long, flowing hair, and a blue trollkin with rings in his ears and a stripe of mane. He holds her around the waist with one arm while she has both hands raised in the air. A beam of bright light emanates from her palms, aimed across the page.

On the other side, below the peak where the two stand together, is a monstrosity.

"It's one of the worms!" I peer closer at the illustration. "Just like in the carving we saw. One of the ancient worms from the desert."

Mom arches a brow at me, then continues patiently. "They lived all over the world." The beam of light is aimed right at the beast, which towers above the two small mortals many times over. "Their caves still run through many hills and mountains. And this worm in particular..."—she taps the page—"is Riggamora, the greatest of them all, and the most destructive."

I squint at it. "This is a fairy tale, Mom."

"Yes, one that originates on the other continent. They still believe in magic there, you know." She gives me a look like I should be aware of all this already. "The evidence exists that Riggamora was, in fact, real. When your father was headed there across the ocean..."

This is an ugly memory for both of us, but she continues on valiantly.

"...it was because he had heard of places where great battles were fought, places where this Riggamora had eaten the very earth, intent on destroying us."

I stare at her. "Dad was after *this*?"

Mom nods slowly, saying nothing.

I'd always known he was pursuing the truth of ancient secrets, that the past had called him across the ocean and the ocean had seen fit to take his life. But I didn't know he was merely chasing myths when he died.

Unable to contain my curiosity, I flip the page in the book. The next illustration shows Riggamora, now a corpse, with humans and trollkin assembled around it.

"Once upon a time, we defeated him," Mom says, caressing the edge of the page with a faraway look in her eyes. She's not thinking about the here and now so much as my father. "What you found may have been a record of that battle. A battle that required one human and one trollkin to protect all of us."

Could those carvings we found have truly depicted a real event?

"And you said you were there by yourself?" Mom asks, doubt in her voice. "The door was simply open?"

I should know by now that I can't hide things from my own mother. She's too smart to believe it was just sitting there waiting to be found.

Collapsing in the chair across from her, I suddenly feel so tired.

"He was there. The orc from before, from the swamp." I clutch my pack close, gripping onto it like a lifeline as I cut the wound open again. "He was... he was sick. Really sick."

I don't know how else to explain what I found. Mom listens silently, nodding her head for me to continue.

"His eyes were purple, and it was like he'd been asleep there for days." I shudder, remembering how his belongings had been scattered everywhere by animals. "We don't know how long."

"We?" Mom echoes.

I rub my cheek surreptitiously. "I woke him up, but I'm not sure how. He was almost delusional." Then I decide I should tell her the whole truth so that perhaps, she can help me decode it. "I was sick, too."

She cocks her head. "The same thing?"

"I felt woozy. Strange. Everything was tinted purple, almost like the magic was taking over my body."

Mom sits back abruptly in her chair, brows creased with worry.

"I felt better almost immediately after I found Graz," I tell her. "It just... went away. And then we found a door. When we both touched it, it opened."

She hums thoughtfully. "Again, it required both of you."

"There's more, though." I can't believe I'm about to tell my own mother what I did. No one was supposed to ever find out, but I want to make sense of it, too. I want to know what happened. I want to share my burden with someone, and if anyone will listen to me and understand me... it's her.

Mom leans forward on her desk. "I'm listening."

When I finish my story, which was utterly humiliating to recount, she's deep in thought. I don't interrupt her. She rises after a time and meanders into the stacks, and I wait patiently until she returns with a rather small, ragged book. She sets it down on the desk between us.

I lean forward to read the title: *Trollkin and Their Strange Habits*. My face heats.

"I read about this phenomenon some years ago," Mom says, tapping her fingers on the desk. "How trollkin can mate for life, imprinting on one another so deeply that it can sometimes have painful, even deadly, side effects."

"What? Side effects?" Squinting at the little book, I pick it up.

"Go home, Vienne. Take it with you."

She's letting me remove a book from the archives? It's so unlike her to let anything this old out of her sight that I'm immediately suspicious.

"I think you have some things to learn." She waves me off with a hand.

There's something comforting in my mother giving me orders, so I agree without complaint, tucking the book into my bag as I hurry out the door.

Chapter 16

VIENNE

I awaken to the sound of my doorknob rattling.

My gun's under my pillow, so I slide my hand under and grab it. I'm in just my underwear, so I slip on some pants and a shirt as someone continues trying to get into my house.

Gun brandished, I sneak toward the door and stay low, so whoever it is can't see in through my window. It's dark, but the moon is shining, allowing me to see the tall figure outside.

"Raiden?" I say aloud, mystified.

"Let me in, Vienne," comes the voice from the other side.

The first thing I think to do is to tuck away the book Mom gave me. I spent some time reading it last night, all written from the point of view of a man who spent most of his life trying to understand trollkin. "The creatures with whom we share this world," as he often referred to them.

I don't need Raiden seeing it, not after I learned what I learned about imprinting. "The mate bond," the author dubbed it. If the constant emptiness in my chest tells me anything, it's that Graz was telling the truth.

But I made an even worse discovery: when one mate dies, there's a high chance the other will, too. Just great. Whatever happens to Graz after this—or to me—we're now tied together.

I twist the doorknob, still holding my gun, and crack the door open. Sure enough, Raiden stands on the other side, his dark hair half covering his eyes.

Dashing and a total asshole. Just my type. Well, before Graz.

"Vienne." Raiden shoves the door open, pushing me aside, and slips into my house. Reflexively I raise my gun and step back. He holds up his hands in surrender.

"You're going to shoot me?" he asks with a sneer. "Your boyfriend?"

My stomach turns over. "You've never been my boyfriend." I lower the gun, even though my instincts rail against it. If I accidentally shot him, I'd go right to jail. "What do you want? Why the fuck are you here in the middle of the night?"

He closes the door behind him with a *click*.

"I'm here about your resignation letter." He fishes something out of his pocket and holds it up. Sure enough, it's the note I wrote before I left. "I didn't give it to anyone, by the way."

I scowl. "Why would you do that? I quit."

"Nobody knows that. I told the rest of the corps you were ill."

There's an odd taste in the air, and all my alarm bells are ringing. I don't put my gun down, but I do keep it at my side, my finger on the trigger.

Raiden takes a step toward me. "What did you find, Vienne? What are you hiding?"

"Nothing," I snap.

He grins like he doesn't believe me for a moment. "You would never just quit. You love the Corps. So you did it for a reason, and I think it's because you discovered something you don't want to share."

"Get out." I flick the safety off my gun so he can hear it. "I've made my decision. Now I need you to leave."

That nasty grin grows even wider. Before I can react, Raiden lunges at me. I shoot my gun reflexively, but it goes right over his shoulder and into the ceiling.

"You shot at me?!" He wraps his arms around mine, pinning them to my sides. I struggle, aiming a kick at his groin, but when my foot connects, he takes it with an angry grunt.

"I always knew you were a piece of shit," I snarl back as I fight him. But Raiden is bigger and meaner, and certainly better trained.

"Didn't stop you from fucking me." He pins me against the wall on my side, then snares both my wrists in one of his hands. With his other hand, he grabs a rope off his belt and winds it around them. Then he kicks me in the back, and a howl of pain leaves my throat as I stumble to my knees.

Fuck. That hurt.

He leans down and speaks into my ear in a deadly voice.

"I raided your apartment while you were gone," he says, his breath hitting my skin and making me cringe. "I found your little map. If you don't want me to kill your mother, you're going to go with me to that last location, and show me what you've found."

"What the fuck do you think it is that it's worth all this?" I try to get to my feet, but Raiden shoves me back down.

"Because I know you, Vienne. Whatever it is, it's big enough that you were willing to give up your life's work." He tugs the rope around my wrists tighter as he crouches down in front of me. "And I want a piece of it."

I glare at him. "It's not treasure."

Raiden shakes his head. "Of course not. You've never been interested in treasure. You like secrets." He reaches out to tap my nose, and I jerk back, tempted to spit on him. "And I know you're keeping a big one."

He yanks me to my feet. It's the middle of the night, so I could scream and perhaps one of my neighbors would come out, but Raiden's dressed in a military uniform. No one would question him dragging a prisoner from their home all tied up.

"If I came back with some ancient discovery, the King would be most grateful, I'm sure," Raiden says, smirking. "Might even get that nice house I've been after."

Damned that old man. He would most certainly reward Raiden handsomely if he came back with magic.

"You fucking asshole," I growl.

Raiden sighs. "The time for talking is over." He grabs a ball of fabric out of his jacket and shoves it roughly into my mouth. "We're headed west, and we leave right now."

GRAZ

The disgust is evident on Gusak's face when I finish telling him the sordid facts—though I left out as much detail as I could. It's likely the exact same face I made when I found Lo'zar in my house, telling me he'd mated with a human.

"But it worked," Gusak muses. "Twice now, it required one human and one trollkin to enter the ruin and access magic?"

I nod, unsure of where he's going with this.

"Hmm." He rises to his feet and paces across the room as he

thinks. "This sickness you described. After she woke you, you said you were well again?"

"Took a while, but yes." I squeeze the arm of the chair I'm sitting in, because this interrogation is making me increasingly uncomfortable.

"And it hasn't returned?" Gusak presses.

I shake my head. "Fit as a fiddle."

"Where are you keeping it?"

Gusak's question confuses me. "Where am I keeping what?"

His expression is dangerous as he says, "The magic. I want to know where you're hiding the rest of it."

I pull out the pendant again. "Right here. It's sealed inside."

Gusak sighs impatiently. "Don't try to lie to me again, Graz, or I'll put you in the pit with Big Green."

I shudder. That's his prize fighter, who could probably tear my head right off my shoulders without much effort.

Closing my eyes, I resign myself to whatever Gusak's going to do with it. I can only hope he'll heed the warnings I've given him so far and not do anything too foolish. "It's in my shop. In a bag, tucked behind some scrap."

"In a *bag*?" Gusak scowls deeply. "You stupid orc. Don't you realize?" He paces over and whacks me, hard, right on the side of the head. I squint and curl my shoulders, hoping to prevent further injuries. "It's poison, you idiot! It was *poisoning* you."

"Poison?" I shake my head. "It's not poison."

"The sickness. You had magic with you, did you not?" Gusak looks ready to cuff me a second time.

I nod hastily. "Yes."

He rolls his eyes. "It's all tied together. I'm surprised someone with your *intellect* hasn't figured it out by now."

Clearly he sees some pattern that I've missed. I think back

to waking up with Vienne's hand on my shoulder, her concerned blue eyes looking into mine.

The fog had cleared, and all I saw was her.

"Vienne." Her name tumbles out of me. "You think it's because of Vienne."

"You were acting strange the first time you came to me," Gusak says, a triumphant look on his face. "I thought it was odd. That's why I tailed you. But you behaved strangely because you had magic on you, isn't it? It was making you ill."

Until Vienne.

"But she cured me." I expel a long, deep breath as I realize the truth for myself. "Why? Why her?"

I don't want to admit it, but I think I already know why.

Then Gusak gives the words life. "Because she's your mate."

Fuck. I know he's right. The mate bond is clearly special to our ancient ancestors, if the vision that Vienne and I shared of the past is true.

Gusak prowls closer to me, no longer pacing. "You know, I have to ask."

The tone of his voice makes me curl my shoulders tight. "Ask anything," I say, even though I fully do not mean it.

"Did you help him?" Gusak is uncomfortably close now, and I sink deeper into my chair. "Were you the one who got that rat Lo'zar out of here on the boat?"

Fuck. I try not to give anything away, but someone like Gusak... he can probably tell the truth just by the expanding of my pupils. Still, he waits for me to answer, his big face and sharp tusks so close that he could gore me.

I have to think about Vienne. Maybe he'll go easier on me —and won't feed me to his pets—since I'm giving up the information willingly.

"...Yes," I finally say. "But I had to."

Gusak leans back, and his brows rise. "Had to? You just *had* to go under your boss's nose and betray him?"

I cringe, but continue anyway. "It wasn't about you," I hurriedly explain. "I had to help my best friend get his mate out of here. Lo'zar saved my life many times over. I owed him."

There. I've said it. I can't take it back now.

But Gusak doesn't summon his guards to take me away, as I expected. When I open my eyes, he's studying me with his arms crossed.

"So this disease can spread. This human-fucking disease." He cocks his head. "You are a clever orc, I'll give you that. I never suspected you. I thought surely that guy is too smart to get involved with something so idiotic and risky."

I have no defense. I knew helping Lo'zar and Rimi would land me into trouble someday, and that day has finally arrived. Maybe Gusak will beat me to a pulp himself. He usually prefers the violence down in his fighting pit, but I've heard he's no stranger to dishing it out, either.

"Mates," the boss hums, suddenly turning away from me. He's not going to cuff me again? Or drag me down to meet the alligators? "So Lo'zar had one, too. In that stupid little human? I lost a lot of money on that deal."

"It was clear they had a bond," I say. I don't know why I'm digging my hole even deeper, but I feel compelled to tell him my reasons. "I've known Lo'zar since I was a boy. I couldn't abandon him."

"Your loyalty is admirable," Gusak says, reaching into his pocket. He withdraws a flip knife, and I realize my time has finally come. I thought I could protect Vienne from this, but I can't.

He approaches me, opening the knife to reveal the silver blade. "But that loyalty should be to me, not him."

"I'm sorry." I'm already doomed, so I might as well tell him the truth. "I've never been loyal to you. I joined the clan because Lo'zar did. I mind my business, and do what you tell me, only so you don't kill me."

Unexpectedly, Gusak barks a loud laugh. He twirls the knife with expert precision.

"You've got balls on you, don't you?" His lip quirks up. "Now that you've left your mate, you don't care what becomes of you anymore."

I shrug. Maybe so. It feels like I left an important part of myself behind in that forest, one that I'll never get back. Perhaps it was my sense of caution and self-preservation.

Gusak gazes at one of the priceless paintings on his wall, as if he's thinking long and hard about what to do with me. Then he turns, approaching me with the knife. I close my eyes and cringe—only to find him cutting free the ropes holding me down to the chair. "Well, you're in luck. As it stands, I need you and your little human *mate*."

I gawk at him. "What for?"

"To get me into the last ruin. So I can see it for myself and decide what must be done with it." He grins, flipping the knife closed and tucking it back in his pocket.

The last ruin. I wonder if Vienne is headed there, too.

I hope not.

Chapter 17

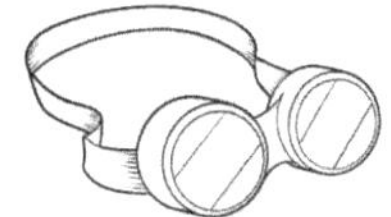

Graz

Gusak wants to go—*personally*. Kal'zan and Agna, the two who found me in the Stoneteeth, are accompanying us.

Even as we prepare for the journey, I still don't believe it. I've never seen the boss leave the clan base before, except on short business trips. Typically he sends someone else to do his dirty work for him, building connections and meeting with partners.

First, though, I build a holding container for the magic I've tucked in the back of my shop under Gusak's orders. He doesn't want it infecting anyone else with my "magic sickness." It takes me quite a while longer to design something robust enough, and he's tapping his toe impatiently the whole time.

Of course, we don't bring any with us. Gusak can't risk getting the sickness himself.

This final marker will be challenging to reach, as it lies

fairly deep in human territory. Perhaps we aren't at war right now, but they will not respond kindly to trollkin in their midst. We'll have to tread carefully and stay hidden.

I think Gusak's generosity has an expiration date, and the moment we open the ruin for him, he might just finally off me for my disobedience. At least he heeded my warning about trying to travel to other locations with the help of magic, and decided he doesn't want to scramble his own brains.

We'll go by train, then get off as close to human territory as we can before taking horses the rest of the way. Gusak has mapped out a trajectory that should avoid any major towns and keeps us off the beaten path.

Though I may not be tied up on this journey, it's clear that I'm his prisoner.

I'm immensely tired of traveling, but I resign myself to it as we board the train. Gusak has a private car with enough beds for all of us, but I still lie awake at night for hours. My soul aches, as if it's been dislodged from my body. It's a misery I've never felt before, and Vienne's orgasmic face as I slid my cock into her, her sweet face as she sleeps at my side, will not leave my mind's eye.

I wonder where she is now. I both hope that I see her at our destination, and that she stays far, far away.

No matter what she's done, I can't let Gusak get his hands on her.

Vienne

Raiden holds casually onto the rope as we ride along, our saddlebags stocked full of supplies. I'm still bound, and the threads dig deeper into my wrists with every day that passes.

We've been on the road for what feels like weeks now. We're going a relatively unpopular direction into more rugged terrain, so we have to ride on horseback the whole way. Raiden refers to my map often, but never asks for my input. He knows I'll lie to him.

The first thing he did was take my gun. All right, sensible. But the moron never second-guessed my full water pouch, and he also hasn't figured out that I don't use it for drinking. It sits in my traveling pack, untouched—if only I could get to it. Even at night, though, Raiden keeps a hold on me, tying my rope around his own wrist so he'll know the moment I move.

Not even my mother knows where I am. If he kills me, no one will ever find out who did it. And I have a suspicion that killing me could very well be on the menu after he gets what he wants.

I can't believe I ever slept with this asshole.

Soon, though, things take a turn for the worse. Raiden ties me to a tree while he sets up camp for the night, and pours out some booze over the tinder to help light it. Just the scent of the alcohol going up in flames evokes a visceral, disgusted response from my stomach. Without any warning, I bend over and puke. Then I sag against the tree when I'm done, panting.

Raiden returns, leaning down to look me in the eyes. "Hm, something upset your tummy?" he says in a mocking tone.

I've always known he was a piece of shit, but I didn't realize the depths to which he'd be willing to sink. He's still wearing his uniform, so no one we pass on the road has questioned why I'm tied up. He simply looks like a lawman taking me off to jail where I belong. And the farther we go, the less often we've encountered other people—and the lower my chance of ever getting away.

"I'm fine," I grind out.

Raiden shrugs. "I'm going to see if I can pinch a rabbit," he says in a bored tone, slinging his rifle over his shoulder as he wanders out into the woods, leaving me there.

I sink down to the ground, hands above my head because the rope won't move. It's pathetic, really, that I'm here, that I haven't found a way out yet. Raiden's certainly not any smarter than I am.

I throw up once more for good measure before he finally comes back. I don't know what's wrong, but it's probably the bad food and the stress has finally caught up to me.

The fire is burning bright and the sun is almost set when Raiden brings his rabbit into camp and skins it before setting it over the flames. Then his hand jerks, abruptly knocking the spit off the rack and sending the raw rabbit tumbling to the forest floor.

"What the fuck?" he mutters, getting up to grab it. He tries to wipe off the dirt. "Fuck!"

That was odd. I watch him closer as he grumbles, pouring water over the carcass and wiping it again, then returning it to the rack.

This time, it's while he's assembling the tent that he shakes again. His arm moves unnaturally, as if the entire thing is twitching involuntarily, and the tent topples over.

Raiden snarls and grabs his own hand, pressing it to his side as if it's a disobedient animal. He mutters something under his breath, clasping the rebellious arm tight.

"What's wrong?" I call out. I just want the chance to mock him after how he's treated me. "Freaking out a little?"

Raiden stiffens. "None of your damned business."

He finishes putting up the tent without further interruption, then begrudgingly gives me some rabbit to eat with my bare hands. I've never been so degraded, but I keep my chin up anyway, shooting him a glare whenever I get the chance.

If he would just let his guard down, maybe I could get to his knife and cut myself loose. Or maybe I could choke him out with the rope while he's asleep. He's been very careful so far, but after whatever strange thing happened to him tonight...he might falter.

I'll have to keep a close eye on him.

Graz

It's not an easy mission for four trollkin to trek across a swath of human territory unseen. I'm starting to wonder if the magic has somehow gotten its claws in him and Gusak has lost his mind.

Kal'zan and Agna kill anyone who comes across us as we make our way through deep forest. Agna keeps us on track with a compass, and somehow, Kal'zan is able to use the stars at night to track our progress. At night, Gusak asks me questions about what I've seen, what experiments I've done, what I've learned about magic. I tell him most of what I know, which still isn't much. But tonight...

"How did you get the rat out of town?" he asks me, rather casually, chewing the bone of a deer we killed a few nights ago and have been lugging around in a cart. "You must have been real clever to sneak a human onto a boat."

I sigh. I expected this, sooner or later, after what I confessed. I'm finally going to have to explain this and reveal my part in all of it. At least I know he won't shoot me before we reach our destination.

"Magic is temporary," I begin. "You make a wish, you impress your desire upon it, and it manifests—for a limited time."

Gusak frowns. "Yeah, so you've told me. Not all that useful."

I hold up a hand. "But it *is* possible to freeze it in time, to stop it from reaching its half-life and dissipating. I've found two ways of doing it."

Gusak sits forward on the log where he's perched. "What are the two ways?" Agna is sharpening her knife, but Kal'zan is also listening from the spot where he's acting as watchdog.

"Well, the first way that Lo'zar discovered was to eat it. That makes whatever you wished for permanent. Then, the magic becomes a part of you."

Gusak's lips screw up with disgust. "He *ate* it?"

"I know. No sense of decency or self-preservation." I pull out my pendant and tap it. "The other way is to build a housing for it that's secured. That way, when you tell it what you want, it holds that command as long as you seal it away before its half-life expires."

I swallow. Here's the ugly part, where I have to tell him exactly how I undermined him.

"I gave Lo'zar an amulet like mine," I continue. "Wear it, and it makes you look... different. It made Rimi, the human, appear like a trolless, so she could get on the boat safely."

Gusak listens with an unreadable expression, but doesn't interrupt.

"It works for him, too," I say, because I can't help myself. I'm proud of the gadget I created for my best friend. "He can appear like a human whenever he needs."

"Impressive." The big orc sits back on his log, tossing his bone away. "And you found all this out yourself through trial and error."

I nod.

"Explains why you got as sick as you did if you were experimenting with it so closely." He rubs his chin. "Trollkin taking human mates. What a bizarre phenomenon. At least now I understand why one of my best men betrayed me." He sighs. "I probably would have done the same."

Is Gusak really admitting this to me? I don't speak, because I don't trust myself.

"Are you still in contact with Lo'zar?" Gusak asks after a time.

I grimace. I do get Lo'zar and Rimi's letters occasionally, though with how he travels, it's hard to respond.

"...Yes." I cringe as I say it. Gusak's too keen to try to bald-faced lie. "He is still working outside the law. And he has a few whelps of his own."

Two, if I remember right. Twins, just born.

Gusak gawks openly at me. "What? Whelps? With a *human*?"

All I can do is nod.

"What a fucking mystery the world is." He rubs his forehead like this has all made him very tired. "I hope you haven't sown a whelp in *your* human."

He sighs and gets up, heading to his tent. I stare at his back as he disappears inside, my mind spinning.

I couldn't have. I couldn't possibly have left my mate behind with a whelp in her belly, all by herself back in that forest.

Could I?

CHAPTER 18

Whatever is happening to Raiden, I'm grateful for it.

I haven't found the perfect opportunity yet to get one over on him, but at least he hasn't noticed my own ailment. I'm constantly battling roiling nausea with a grimace on my face, and my whole body is sore and aching. I can barely eat, and all food tastes like trash left out in the sun.

This can't be the same thing as before. No, that sickness was different—it's what's happening to Raiden right now, with his body behaving in strange ways. I see him squinting, as if struggling to see what's ahead of him, leaning forward on his horse to get a better look. He's tired more often, stopping early at night to make camp because he's too exhausted. Once, he even lost his balance and nearly fell over.

Embarrassing I haven't gotten away yet, but I'm distracted, too.

I don't know how close we are to our destination because he won't let me see the map, but it's almost as if I can *feel* it nearby, like there's a tether tied around me and someone on the other end is tugging on it, drawing me closer. Perhaps we only have a day left, if that buzzing awareness behind my eyes is any indication.

That night, after Raiden falls asleep next to me, my rope tied around his arm, I stare up at the night sky and dig deep for an answer to my conundrum. I need a way out of this, before Raiden gets what he wants and doesn't have a use for me any longer.

But no matter how I hope, no matter what solution I think of, nothing changes.

The worst part is the knowing. After this many days, I'm not just ill from undercooked meat. I don't have to be an idiot to figure out what's wrong with me. When one of the other members of the Corps found herself pregnant, she also heaved up perfectly good food and felt sick to her stomach constantly, until she had to turn around and head home before she could complete the mission.

I told myself that would never be me. Raiden has always pulled out, and when I was with him, I was careful to drink my purentea. The last thing I wanted was to destroy my reputation with the Corps by having my boss's kid.

But after I left home, there was no reason to bring tea along with me, and I didn't even think twice about it when I let Graz fuck me senseless over and over again. Because why would I? He's trollkin. An orc. A monster. Perhaps our bodies fit together, but that in itself was a miracle. I couldn't have imagined we were... *compatible*.

Now I think I might have been wrong. I know exactly whose child I'm carrying now, and it turns my stomach even more sour.

Graz left me. He abandoned me there after everything he said to me. He's not trustworthy, and he'll never accept us.

My child will grow up without a father, just like I did.

I finally manage to fall asleep, tormented by an uncertain and increasingly perilous future.

Graz

I am haunted.

As we get closer to our destination, the dread winds up even stronger in my belly.

I filled up Vienne over and over, making sure she was utterly drenched in me. The chance I've left her carrying my whelp is horribly high. Why did I never consider it? Why didn't I stop myself?

I wish I could reach her somehow, but all my magic is back in the shop. There's nothing I can do. I just have to hope somehow, we find each other again.

Human settlements grow few and far between as we advance. The landscape begins to slope upward, bringing us ever closer to the massive peak in the distance, where Gusak is convinced we'll find the final site.

I wonder what he'll do when we get there. I've tried to ask, but for him, it "depends on what's there." That's all I get.

Another day passes, and at last, we're at the base of the peak.

"It must be inside this mountain," Gusak says thoughtfully as we study the climb ahead of us, securing our packs. There are no signs of civilization within our immediate vicinity, so I'm inclined to agree. The last site was well-hidden, too. I only hope we can get inside it without Vienne's help.

Gusak sends Agna and Kal'zan to scout, and we start the climb up, hoping that one of us will stumble across the entrance. But there's no sign of it, even as they return to the campfire that night. I start to wonder if perhaps the map is incorrect, and we're looking in the wrong place.

The next morning, we leave the horses and cart behind to ascend the mountain. We fight with heavy boulders and slopes of scree, but as we climb higher, I catch sight of something that gives me hope: a ledge sits above us, clearly carved into the stone by intelligent hands.

"There!" I call out. Gusak follows where I'm pointing, then picks up his pace, climbing on ahead of me with a strength I didn't realize he possessed while Agna and Kal'zan bring up the rear.

The way is perilous, but at last, we reach the ledge. It is the first of many that seem to lead even higher up the mountain.

Gusak adjusts his pack. "Here we go." There's a surprising eagerness on his face. "Ready?"

I nod. "Ready."

We start the final ascent, climbing from one ledge to the next. Agna nearly falls, but Kal'zan is able to steady her in time.

We're all out of breath by the time we reach the last ledge, which is more of a platform. And here, recessed into the mountainside, is a doorway.

I could simply collapse with my relief and my exhaustion, but now that we've gotten to our destination, there's still more to go.

Pulling my lamp out of my bag, I light it on the understanding that I'll go first. I wade into the darkened doorway, holding the lamp up high, while Gusak follows along behind me.

Like the other ruins I've visited, carvings line the walls, written in the same ancient language we've seen before.

"Do you know what any of this means?" Gusak asks, pausing to examine them.

I shake my head. "Not a clue." I wonder if Vienne's mother ever discovered their meanings, and my chest tightens painfully.

He *hmm*s as we continue on, deeper into the mountain. I shudder as we progress, wondering what would happen if it collapsed around us. It's already happened once, and I barely got out with my life. I feel like I'm being squeezed in from all sides, and my breathing speeds up.

A hand lands on my shoulder. "Keep it together, bookworm," Gusak growls.

I swallow and nod, then continue on.

Soon, to my great satisfaction, I catch sight of purple light up ahead. The idea of Gusak getting his hands on some magic of his own is a terrifying thought, but that fear is momentarily overwhelmed by the thrill of finding what I set out to find.

I pick up my pace and so does Gusak, until we're jogging toward it. At last, the hallway ends. I step out from under the low overhang to find a rather small room carved into the rock. Purple magic lights up carvings all along the walls, every last surface decorated with them.

Gusak freezes, inhaling sharply at the sight of it.

"It's just like you said, bookworm." He grins, approaching one of the carvings with a hand outstretched. He examines the same image I've seen in every ruin I've visited: the human and the trollkin faces staring into one another's eyes. "I wonder if it's dangerous just standing here at all." He snorts. "Too late now."

But the engraving is all there is. The room is too small to hide much, and I see nothing that would indicate another door or passageway.

Then I spot it: the two pairs of handprints on the wall.

"Fuck." I beeline toward them, kneeling to get a better look. "We can't open it." I hang my head, putting my hands on both handprints. "I need Vienne."

Gusak says nothing as he takes off his pack. He fishes around in it, then withdraws something I'd never thought I'd see: a few sticks of dynamite.

"Maybe we can force our way through."

Vienne

Today, we're ascending. The map appears to be guiding us toward a huge peak in the distance. There aren't others around it—it's simply a lone mountain among the hills.

I wonder if, once upon a time, it was a volcano. The top appears as if someone sliced the tip right off.

Raiden's illness is getting worse. By the time the sun sets, he's shivering all over though the weather is anything but cold. When we bed down that night in silence, he ties my rope around his hand—but fails to double-knot it.

My heart speeds up. Not noticing what he's done, Raiden lies down beside me and rolls over, showing me his back.

When I'm certain that he's fallen asleep, I ever-so-gently tug on my rope. Raiden grunts, but doesn't wake up, as the knot loosens. I tug again, hoping against hope he's conked out enough not to notice.

The rope falls free and tumbles to the ground. Raiden snorts, staying asleep.

I suck in a breath. I don't have long, and I need to get as far ahead of him as possible. But I also don't want to risk waking him up by taking his supplies, so I simply grab my own pack off the ground, put it over my back, and step away from the campsite. The horses watch me curiously, but if I'm heading up the mountainside, I don't need a horse.

I have to find the magic before Graz or Raiden do. That's my only goal now.

Taking a deep breath, I square my shoulders, turn toward the peak, and take off at a run.

I keep going as long as I can, trying to put distance between us. Eventually my run slows to a jog, and then a walk as I recover my breath. Raiden hasn't allowed me to eat much, so I don't have a lot of fuel to go on.

I stop briefly to devour some rations and drink water. I still have the skin full of magic, and briefly I wonder if I should use it. I want to make sure I'm going the right direction.

Pulling out the water skin, I open the lid and pour some glowing purple magic into my hand.

"Show me where to go," I murmur to it. "Where is the site?"

The magic glows brighter, rising up off my palm. It spreads and flattens, until it ceases to glow, and a map falls into my hands. When I peer down at it, a bright purple marker appears, then another one.

As I start climbing, one of the markers begins to move. That must be me—and the other marker, up ahead, is my destination. I follow the path with my eyes, and sure enough, it's taking me up the side of the mountain.

I put the water skin away and tuck the map under my arm. It's going to be a tough climb, but I know I can do it. I have to do it. I have to reach the last location and secure its treasure, so no one else can find it.

Especially not the trollkin.

Putting my head down, I start the ascent. I'm still sick to my stomach, but I push through, climbing over one rock and then another. Eventually, the map disappears.

I will make it to the top, and resolve this once and for all.

But by the time I'm halfway up, I'm panting and sweating in the full heat of the morning. No—I have to keep going. I can't let Raiden catch up to me.

I climb and climb, irritated at how weak my body has become. Then, up above, I spot an outcropping in the rock. It's high, but I think I can get to it without falling.

Creeping up the sheer cliffside, I finally reach it and pull myself up and over the top. I lie there, desperately trying to bring air back into my lungs.

Wait. Up ahead there's another ledge like this one. Excitement rushes through me as I peer up, finding more ledges.

I've made it. But I don't have time to rest, not until I find the last clue.

CHAPTER 19

"Don't!" I rush to grab the dynamite out of Gusak's hands, but he holds them just out of my reach.

"Calm down, bookworm." He flaps his hand far too cavalierly. "This will do the job. We'll set it, then exit the way we came in."

"It will bring the whole mountain down!" I could just punch him. "And who knows what would happen if you blew up the magic? I've seen the damage it can do."

Gusak studies me with suspicious eyes. "You don't want me to find it, do you?"

I snarl in frustration. Sure, that's part of it. But I don't think the ruin will be here at all if he blows a charge inside it.

"Don't be an idiot," I say rather boldly. Gusak has a gun on him, and so do the others. But I can't let him do this. "The tunnel will collapse, and we'll all die in this dark place under rubble."

"Then what do you propose?" the boss snaps. "There's no other way in without your little human."

I wish I had a better answer, but I don't. As much as I wish I could see her again, as long as my soul clamors to be near hers, this would be the poorest moment for her to arrive. Gusak would slap her in chains and use her for his own purposes, and then who knows what he'd do with her afterward?

"Boss," Agna pipes up. "I think we have company."

Gusak whips out his gun, and we turn to face the tunnel where Agna is watching our backs. All three of them position their weapons, ready to shoot whoever might appear.

Then a small person, a familiar person, emerges from the darkness. She has cropped yellow hair and bright blue eyes, so piercing they shine even in the low light.

Fuck.

Vienne comes to an abrupt halt when she sees what's waiting for her. She holds up her hands, backing up the way she came.

"Don't you dare," snarls Gusak, and even though she can't understand him, she obeys, coming to a stop.

Vienne? I use my thoughts to say her name.

That's when she notices me standing a few paces behind the boss, holding the lantern. Her eyes narrow.

You? What are you doing here with... them? Her brows lower in suspicion. *I knew it. I knew you would lead them right to it.*

I didn't have a choice, I snap back. *It was that or be killed.*

Maybe you should have let them kill you. Her eyes are hard as flint.

It hurts, I won't deny it. My mate is standing in front of me again, and I want nothing more than to throw my arms around her, to kiss her all over, to make sure she's well. But I don't think that would be welcomed by anyone.

"Stop it," Gusak barks when we've remained silent for too long. "What is she saying?"

"She wishes I were dead," I say grimly.

"Hmm. Not the reunion I expected." Gusak tilts his head. "Well, she's here now. What good luck." He nods in Kal'zan's direction. "Tie her up. Now we can finally get into this place."

I want to object, to tell him he doesn't need to do that, but it'll fall on deaf ears. He doesn't trust a human, and I'm not sure that I trust her, either.

But seeing her with my own eyes again, everything in my chest pulls tight, so tight I almost can't breathe. I need her in my embrace, and it's like every moment I don't have her is another nail in my soul.

Kal'zan snatches Vienne's arm roughly, and I growl as he jerks her toward him. Vienne lets out a squawk, and shouts what's obviously a curse in her own language.

What are they doing? she demands of me, her eyes flashing with anger.

What does it look like? I should be kinder, but the relief at seeing her again twines with the sense of betrayal I left with.

Vienne snarls as Kal'zan ties both of her wrists together. *Out of one cookpot and into another.*

What do you mean? I ask. *How did you get here?*

She simply shoots me a deadly glare as Kal'zan leads her into the room. Gusak points at the handprints on the wall.

"Right there," he says. "You too, Graz."

Nodding in understanding, I follow them. Vienne struggles against her bonds as she's forced to kneel, and Kal'zan turns her so he can press her hand to the handprint there. I want nothing more than to free her, but I don't want Gusak to turn on her.

I knew you would spill the secret, Vienne says, her voice defeated. *Now we're all doomed.*

She closes her eyes as I crouch beside her. I hesitate just before putting my hand on the print.

Vienne. I try to get her to look at me, but she refuses. *I didn't mean for this to happen.*

Her answer is silence, her gaze pinned straight ahead.

I swallow as I press my hand to the wall, and the moment I do... the earth all around us rumbles.

Kal'zan stumbles, dropping Vienne's rope. Before any of us can react, she yanks her wrists apart, pulling the rope free. She dives for Kal'zan, tackling him to the ground while the rest of us try to get our feet under us. In a flash of motion, she gets her hand around his gun and pulls it free of his holster.

Our handprints depress into the stone, and the floor shifts. Vienne jumps to the side as the rock right under her feet slides open.

Now there's a hole with purple light spilling out, illuminating the whole room. Less than a second later, Vienne has the barrel of her gun aimed at my face.

I hold up my hands as I fall onto my ass. Gusak's managed to get to his feet again, but no one moves as Vienne keeps her weapon pointed at me.

Tell them to let me go, or I shoot you.

She would kill me to get what she wants. I swallow down just how much it aches. The bond between us must only go one way if that's what she's willing to put on the line.

They won't care if you shoot me, I tell her. *You'll just be sealing your fate.*

"Once again, not how I expected this to go," Gusak muses, taking a step toward her.

Vienne shakes her gun and hollers something threatening in her language. *Tell him to stop.*

But Gusak doesn't care if she puts a bullet through my

brain now that the door is open. So Vienne pivots, aiming the gun at him, instead.

Gusak comes to a stop.

"I guess we're at an impasse," he says, his face betraying nothing as he nods at me. "I thought you said she was your mate. Can't you do anything?"

I bite my lip. If she shot Gusak... it could solve some problems for me, but then we'd still have to deal with Kal'zan and Agna.

You can't win, I say to Vienne, putting as much certainty into the words as I can. *You could take him out, but what about the two others?*

I'll kill them all. Her hand is shaking, her expression fierce and vengeful. *I have something to protect.*

What does she mean by that?

He's not going to give it to the Grand Chieftain, I say, hoping I can convince her to stand down. *He knows better than to touch it. It can make you... very sick.*

Vienne's eyes briefly travel to me before going back to Gusak.

Sick?

Remember when you found me passed out? I remind her. *Like that. Too much exposure to magic makes you sick. I don't know what it does after extended exposure, but... he's afraid of it.*

A sort of clarity registers in her expression.

Like Raiden. She frowns. *Raiden is sick, too.*

Who?

Vienne presses her lips into a thin line, clearly not keen to fill me in. Keeping the gun trained on Gusak, she gestures to me.

Get down there, she says, indicating to the hole in the floor. *We get to it and destroy it before he can do anything terrible.*

Slowly I rise to my feet, considering her plan. If she shoots at Gusak, she's dead. And I can't let them gun my mate down, so that means following her orders.

"What are you doing?" snaps Gusak as I move toward the hatch that's opened in the floor.

"She wants me to destroy it, or she'll kill you."

Gusak rolls his eyes. "I know you don't care that much about my life."

I ignore him as I move to the hatch and peer into it. A great pool of magic lies underneath us, a good way down. Taking a deep breath to steady myself, I scoot my legs over the edge. I don't know how far it is, but I'll have to take the risk.

Hanging from my hands, I drop the rest of the way to the floor. My feet absorb most of the shock of landing, but it still hurts like a bitch.

I'm in, I say to Vienne.

Her feet appear overhead, and she slides over the edge and drops like it's nothing. When she lands, her beautiful face is illuminated by the glowing purple magic.

She points her gun at me, and her blue eyes are like razors.

You know what to do.

VIENNE

Every part of me aches, seeing him again. I want nothing more than to throw myself at him, to have him touch me every place he touched me before, to bury my face in his chest and inhale how wonderful he smells.

But I can't let my feelings get the better of me. I have a mission here, and I need to do it before Raiden catches up to us. Then, somehow, I have to get out of this situation alive.

I'm responsible for more than just me now.

Overhead, the trollkin are yelling at one another, peering down over the side with their own weapons in hand. We don't have time.

I gesture at the pool of magic with my gun. *Poison it,* I tell Graz, trying to keep my voice firm even as I want to fall apart. He brought others here. He spilled the secret, and now I have even more reasons why this place needs to be gone. *We're going to take this mountain down, too.*

Before he can answer, though, the stone rumbles once again. This time I'm prepared, digging in my heels and remaining steady even as the whole ruin around us moves. Then, overhead, the hole in the stone where we entered starts closing.

"No!" I shout. Fuck. I can't get trapped in here. I can't die in here.

I rush to the pool of magic, climbing up onto the stone rim, hoping I can find us a way out. But the hatch closes in mere seconds, and everything goes completely dark—except for the bright pool, and the carvings in the walls around us.

No, no, no! I lean down to gather up magic in my hands. *I can't be stuck like this!*

I pour the magic out of my hands, all while Graz watches. I make my wish: to open that stone door and let us back out.

Nothing happens.

A hand lands on my shoulder, and—scared out of my skin—I leap two feet away, spinning around to aim my gun at my attacker.

Graz doesn't even raise his hands up as I point it right in his face. He stands there, arms at his sides, a horrible sadness in his eyes.

Vienne. You're not going to kill me, are you?

I'm breathing much too fast, but I can't slow the furious beating of my heart. What if we never get out of here? I've never felt claustrophobic before now, but it's too much. It's all too much. Even if we do escape, there are three big, armed trollkin waiting, and somewhere, Raiden is on his way.

And that's just the tip of the iceberg. What lies underneath, all the things I can't say and can't feel—

Vienne? Graz's brows crease. *What's wrong?*

Nothing! I would never shoot him. Not Graz. Not *my* Graz.

I hate how much just seeing him has reduced me to this trembling damsel.

He takes a step toward me, and then another, until the barrel of my weapon is right between his eyes and I can almost feel his breath on me.

Do it, he says. *If you really want to.*

Of course I don't want to. It's just all I have to defend myself with against this onslaught of emotion.

You left me. I practically snarl the words out. *Why shouldn't I? You lied through your teeth. You told me all these pretty things, and then you left.*

I back away from him, lowering the gun. I need to put space between us again. I need to reclaim my sanity.

I can't let you do what you want to do, Graz says, voice soft. *I can't, Vienne. I'm sorry. I understand why you—*

I'm the one with the gun, I interrupt. But we both know there's no force behind it. I couldn't do that to the father of my kid. Just the thought fills me with nausea, and my knees almost buckle under me.

Graz's arm darts out, curling under me, righting me again. I try to push him away, but he doesn't let go.

There's something wrong. Graz nudges me toward the edge of the pool, lowering me until I'm sitting against it. I don't have the wherewithal to push him away. *Vienne, tell me what's going on.*

I hate him. I hate him so much right now that I don't want

to share this precious nugget of truth with him. But I also need him, so badly, and I must know that baby is going to make it out of this alive.

Falling forward, I cover my face with my hands.

I'm pregnant, I finally say. It's like dropping a boulder I didn't realize I'd been carrying. *I'm pregnant, Graz. With your child.*

CHAPTER 20

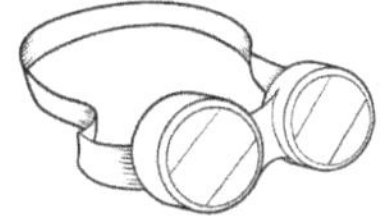

The words circle around in my head, over and over, so fast I feel almost dizzy.

My little mate is carrying my whelp.

Poor Vienne, holding onto a secret like this all on her own, keeping it close to her chest as it guides all of her actions. She will be a fierce and protective mother, I already know that. Like a bear and its cub. I just need to make sure she gets out of here alive.

I think I knew it before she said the words, as if I could feel our whelp winking into life. Perhaps I can already sense that small seed growing inside my mate's belly.

But she detests me. I've ruined the bond we had, shattered it into smithereens when I left her behind that day. I let my own emotions rule me, too. Now, I don't know if the bridge between us can be repaired.

I sure as hell am going to try.

That is incredible, I say to her as I sit beside her. *A marvel of the universe.* Tentatively I slip an arm around her shoulders, but instantly, she jerks back. Her blue eyes are as sharp as daggers as she glares up at me.

You made it clear what I am to you. She scoots away, putting distance between us. *You don't get to say that. We're not going to be some happy family. I'm destroying this place, and if I can get out alive, I'm going home.*

I shudder all over, imagining that. She would keep my whelp from me?

Of course, I can't blame her. I told her in no uncertain terms that she is now alone. Can I possibly convince her she's not? No matter what she does, no matter how I disagree with her choices, I can't stay away from her. I can't let her go on by herself, bearing this burden on her own. I won't live a life without my mate and our whelp. It would tear me apart from the inside out, as it has since we last parted ways.

If I'm going to be a father, I'm going to do it as well as I can. I'm going to be there for her, support her and hold her. And when my whelp is born, I'll make sure they are both safe and sound.

And I will not give that up, no matter what.

I'm so sorry, Vienne. I slide off the ledge and fall to my knees in front of her. *I was angry. Discovering magic, finding the truth behind it, that's all that's mattered to me.*

She frowns deeply. *I know. That's all you care about. I care about saving the world, and keeping magic* out *of the hands of goons like that.*

No, you don't know what I care about. I give her a firm, staid look. *You don't understand at all what you mean to me. How much I've missed you. How much I need you.*

Her lips purse like she doesn't believe me.

You brought others here, she snaps. *Now the Grand Chieftain is going to find out, and we will all be doomed—*

Gusak is too selfish to do that, I tell her. *If anything, he'll want keep it for himself.*

She glares at me. *That's even worse! Who is that guy? What does he want?*

I shrug, because I genuinely don't know the answer. What would Gusak do with this kind of power at his disposal?

He's my boss, I finally say. *I'm... I'm a part of a clan. A crime syndicate. I had no choice but to bring him here, or he'd kill me.*

She sneers. *Maybe you should've let him kill you.*

She's angry, and that's the only reason I don't let the words into my heart. My mate is sharp-tongued while still sensitive. I've hurt her deeply, just like she hurt me. But I understand now that she did what she thought was right.

I gently place my hands on her knees, and though she trembles under them, she doesn't push me away. The pain and hatred in her face falters for just a moment, and that's the clue I need to be certain she still feels something for me, even if it's only a thin thread.

I had to live so I could see you again. I run my hands soothingly up and down her thighs. *You're all I've wanted since I walked away.*

More pretty words, she says with a grumble.

True words, though. It doesn't matter what you did. I should have stuck by you and worked through it with you.

Vienne glares down at me, but there's less venom in her eyes than before.

I don't know how we get out of here, I say, glancing up at the closed hatch in the ceiling, *but when we do, I am not leaving your side. Ever.*

Her scowl softens. *You say that now.*

And I mean it. You and the whelp are mine. *And I'm going to do whatever I have to do to keep it that way.*

There's a split second when her mask melts, and I think I've gotten through to her.

Vienne. I know we're different, and you have no reason to trust me now. I look her in the eyes, demanding that she look back at me and see my truths. *But I want you. Only you. I want to live a life with you, raise our whelp together, and keep both of you safe.*

She turns her head away. *I can do that myself. I can take care of us on my own.*

I have to smile. *I know you can. But I want to. I want to be the one you come to. I want to be there while you go through this.*

Her shoulders slump, and abruptly, Vienne falls forward, collapsing.

Stop it, she whimpers. *Stop saying what I want to hear.*

I'm saying what I want to say. I'm saying what I really feel. Can you hear me?

Cautiously I reach out to her, wrapping my big arms around her much tinier body. When Vienne doesn't flinch or fight, I drag her off the edge of the pool and down into my lap. But as she lies limp there, it's almost as if she is boneless. As if she's given up.

I hold her close, bundling her tight against me so she knows I'm here to help carry her onward.

Vienne

Why does it feel so good to be with him again? It's like a missing part of my soul clicked back into place, and now all I can do is sink into his arms hoping I don't drown.

Graz seems so confident we'll find a life outside of this mess, I almost let myself believe in the same thing. A world where we could be together, where we could have a family together? I want that world, but I'm not sure it exists.

You know, he says quietly, stroking my hair as he cradles me to his chest. *I have a friend who is mated to a human, too.*

My head jerks up. *What? There are more?*

He nods. *Not just them, either. They've heard of others, out in the world, besides us. Maybe we could find them.*

Who is this 'friend'?

He laughs at the tone of my question. *He was very close to me growing up. I used magic to help the two of them get out of the city safely. They're out there somewhere, with whelps of their own.*

So we're not the only ones. I peer down at where Graz's hands are wrapped around my belly. *There could be a life out there for us.*

If we can get out of here without that other big orc taking us out. I've already shown myself to be hostile, and I don't think a guy in charge of a crime syndicate will take kindly to what I've done.

How do we escape this mess? I ask him. *My own boss... he's headed here, too.*

Graz blinks at me. *Your boss?*

It's a long story. I flinch, thinking about my past with Raiden, the fact that I even let him touch me once upon a time. *He dragged me out here, and I just barely managed to get away. He's losing his mind, I think. That magic sickness. I don't know how long we have until he makes it up the mountain.*

Graz sighs. *It's coming at us from all directions.* He lowers his head until it's resting on my shoulder, and he breathes in deeply. *It will work out, though. I know it will.*

I want to believe his assurances, but nothing has turned out the way I thought it would.

How do we get out of here? I ask, searching the ceiling for any sign. *I already wished, and it did nothing.*

Maybe magic will tell us, he suggests. *Like it did last time. You think we need to just wait?*

He nuzzles the back of my neck with his nose. *Or do what we did last time.*

My body heats up just at the mention of it.

You smell so damned good, Graz murmurs, squeezing me tighter. *I've been dreaming about it, how you smell.*

It soothes me, knowing I still affect him the way he does me. I settle fully into him, nested in the shelter of his lap. He runs his nose over the shell of my ear, his breath on my skin making all the tiny hairs stand up on end.

I dreamt about you, too, I confess. *Too much.*

Mmm, you thought about me? Something is already developing between Graz's thighs that I can feel underneath me. *What did you think about?*

I know what he's doing, but I want the same thing, and I'm too tired to fight it. We can't escape this place, and all I want right now is to get lost in my orc, to forget that everything beyond this room even exists.

Maybe, for this short moment, I can pretend.

Well, I thought about your cock. I grin when he chuckles against my throat, then kisses there. The cool brush of his tusks on my skin makes me feel utterly alive. *And the way you looked at me when...*

Ah, when I made love to you? The way the words roll through my mind, I shiver all over.

If that's what you want to call it. I'm surprised it translates the way it does, but they must have two words for these things, as well.

It is. That's what it was. One of his hands adventures upward, under the swell of my chest, and I allow it. *You know it, too. We did it the way that mates do.*

I know he's right, now. I know because I couldn't stand

walking away from him, because it would break me if we were separated again.

Covering his hand with mine, I squeeze, forcing his own fingers to apply more pressure to my breast. Graz groans behind me, that lump between his legs surging against my ass. He rubs my nipple with surprising force, and I bend into him, unable to hold up the barrier between us for even a moment longer.

Vienne, he murmurs, low and velvety. *Do you know what you do to me? What just touching you does to me?* His other hand, still around my waist, pushes me down so I'm grinding against his groin. I gasp at the sensation of just how thick and full he's gotten for me in a few moments. *I want nothing but you.*

This time, a moan escapes me as he nips at my neck and his palm winds down between my legs. He applies pressure there, over the fabric of my pants, and the friction is delicious.

So warm. Graz lets out a hum of pleasure. *I bet you're already wet for me under there.*

I wriggle against him knowing he's right, and everything that happened in that cave is coming back to me now, reminding me just how much I need him.

He plucks open the buttons of my pants, and once they're loose, he slides his fingers down inside them. It's like a dam breaking open, the way my need overtakes me the moment his hand reaches my center.

Graz, please. I buck my hips up against his intrusion, begging for him to touch me more. Maybe I'm a pathetic woman going back for another sip, but I can't help myself. We're magnetized together, and I won't truly be free until I have him again.

He makes a thoughtful sound as he drags the pad of his finger through the swollen petals of my pussy, pausing when he reaches my clit. *Absolutely soaked for me,* he says as he tests it, gentle and light with his touch.

I am. I'm simply alight, my blood pounding fast and my pulse thrumming in my throat as he moves so slowly, so intentionally, swirling his finger about in circles as if he knows exactly what touch I like, what touch I need. Unexpectedly, a whimper falls out of me, and Graz nips the shell of my ear.

Do you want more? Teasingly he swoops down, pressing the tip of his finger inside me. My head falls back against his shoulder as he retreats, playing with my clit again. My hips start to roll in time with his movements as he sets off a spark inside me, a spark that catches the tinder on fire when he sinks his finger in deep.

So small. I gasp as he curls it, stroking along my inner wall. Oh, fuck. I clench all over, and he chuckles against me. *So sensitive, too. It will feel so good when my cock is inside you.*

Just the suggestion makes me moan. *Don't make me wait forever.*

Graz chuckles against me. *I won't.* He slides his hands under me, lifting me up as he gets to his feet. He sets me on the ground, but he's still caressing my ass and reaching between my legs.

Bend over. Take these off.

Every inch of my skin trembles at the command in his voice. I kick off my pants, and with my shirt still on, I hurriedly prop my hands on the edge of the pool, keeping my legs straight so my ass is up in the air.

There we are, Graz croons. He positions himself behind me, still playing with me, taunting me. Then I hear his suspenders snap, and his hand leaves me for just a moment.

It's soon replaced by something else, something much broader. Graz groans as he drags the head of his cock all over me, rubbing my clit with it until I'm pathetically shoving my hips back against his. I can almost feel his self-satisfied smirk, though I can't see his face.

He leans over me, and finally, he guides himself to that needy, wet place that's begging for him. But he merely hovers there, applying the faintest pressure as he smears me with his spill.

Tell me, he says, even as I try to shunt my hips back against his. *Tell me what you want, Vienne.*

I look at my own reflection in the pool of purple, glowing magic. My hair is mussed, my cheeks darkened, my lips parted with each of my heavy breaths.

You, I finally say, dropping my head into the circle of my arms. *I want you, Graz. I want all of you.*

With a grunt, he gives me what I'm asking for.

CHAPTER 21

VIENNE

A cry tumbles out of me as Graz slowly, gently, smoothly pushes himself in.

Oh, fuck, I'm tight. It's been too long, and I'm not open enough for him yet. With just the head of his cock seated inside me, Graz groans, halting there.

I forgot how small you are, he mutters, pulling back just slightly, and then pushing in again as far as he can—which isn't far. I bite my lip, bracing at the delicious stretch, willing myself to allow him in. I need him again, more than I need air.

Graz palms the cheeks of my ass as he continues his slow progress, squeezing his fat cock in until my body refuses, then pulling back out again, blowing on the simmering coals of my pleasure.

You're so wet for me, he murmurs, bending over me. He reaches a hand down between us, wetting his fingers, then using it to glance over my clit.

I seize up all over, and he groans behind me as he shoves himself through it, forcing me open wider for him.

Oh, yes, yes, please, I find myself chanting as he rubs me, still remaining shallow as my body adjusts to him. *I need it, I need it.*

He chuckles above me, his hand smoothing up my back as he tests even deeper waters. He's so tuned in with me, it's as if we're two instruments playing in perfect harmony while he gives me only what I can take. My arms are shaking underneath me, trying to hold me up against the pool, as Graz offers even more of himself.

Barely halfway inside you. Graz speeds up his attack on my clit as he pulls back and then fills me again. I'm so close already, vibrating with the need to climax, that all it takes to push me over the edge is one more firm stroke, and then I'm crying out as I erupt. I clamp down tight, and Graz moans behind me, slamming into me again and again as my head spins wildly. My arms give out, and I fall against the edge of the pool panting.

Ah, Graz says with a smug tone. *So ready for me.* He gently leaves my clit, grabbing both cheeks of my ass in his hands as he continues fucking me, slowly, languidly. I come down from my orgasm only to find more building as he pumps inside me, reaching an even greater depth than before. I don't know how much my body can take, but the exquisite satisfaction of being together again overwhelms everything.

Mother of my whelp, he moans as he thrusts shallowly again, clearly intent on winding me up. *My mate for all time.*

His words sing in my mind, wrapping me up in a soft blanket. I never considered any of these things—my romantic future, having children—because it never fit into my plan. But now, that's the only life I want.

And then, finally, Graz is fully sheathed in me, right where he belongs.

You feel incredible, I manage to think, my whole body taut as a wire. *Fuck me, please. Make me remember.*

He leans down over me, kissing down my neck and shoulders.

Whatever she wants. Graz reels back, then buries himself in me again, our bodies back where they belong at last. He ratchets up his pace, plundering me for all I'm worth, that huge cockhead stimulating everything inside me, sending sharp tendrils of bliss all over my body. I'm helpless under him, a willing and boneless recipient as he snarls above me and plunges into me in a punishing rhythm.

I'm going to fill you up all over again, he says, and I can feel his nails as he squeezes my ass. *And when you've had this whelp, I'm going to put another one in you, and another.*

Oh, fuck. I'm whining, jerking and twitching with every thrust, his vision for the future washing over me. A life where that's possible? I can't imagine it, and yet I want it in my claws.

Graz grunts, his breath heavy against my neck as he takes me harder, faster, his nails scraping down my back. I'm so close again, I could simply combust.

Graz! I'm writhing, calling out his name. *I'm... I'm...* I can't even think a complete sentence as he touches that same sensitive place over and over. He groans above me as his cock starts to thicken and swell, and I can't take it anymore.

I wail as my finish is ripped out of me, a feeling that completely overshadows everything. I forget where we are, why we are, and I'm consumed in nothing but Graz.

Graz

My mate's cunt milks me so wonderfully that I have no choice but to release. I slam into her again as my balls tighten, as every vein in my body burns with my fiercely rushing blood. I roar as my seed shoots out of me, splashing her sweet cunt, filling her so full it drips out of her all around my cock.

Panting, I nearly collapse on top of her, my legs trembling under me. I shiver all over, the sheer force of my pinnacle sucking all the strength out of my body.

I dip a hand into the pool of magic while Vienne gasps for air against the rim. Then I spill it onto the floor, telling it what I want: a soft place for my mate and I to rest.

Instantly, it responds, glowing brightly as it spreads and inflates, until there's a broad mattress covered in soft furs and pillows. Gently, I withdraw from Vienne's small body, and even more of my seed spills from her well-used cunt. I lift her into my arms, and she willingly allows me to carry her to the bed, where I set her down. Her skin is blotchy red, her lips parted as she breathes heavily. Then I lie next to her, rolling over to wrap her up in my arms.

She tilts her head up to look at me, and I seize her chin before planting my lips on hers.

Mmm, she murmurs sleepily, accepting my kiss. She simply melts against me, letting me swallow her up as I devour her delicious mouth. When I pull away, Vienne's eyes are closed, her breaths already slowing. My poor mate is so worn out from worrying, from traveling, from her body changing, that she is already halfway to dreams.

Pulling her in tight to my side, I let my head fall to the pillow. Still, our lovemaking did not open our way out. This ruin must not behave like the others.

I try not to consider that we might be trapped here forever as I fall asleep beside her.

When I awaken, though, I open my eyes to find a bright moon shining down on us. I squint, peering all around to see we are now lying in the grass on a hillside, Vienne still sleeping peacefully at my side.

I blink a few times, trying to figure out how we ended up here. The last thing I remember, we were trapped inside a mountain and had fallen asleep on a magic bed.

Disentangling myself gently from Vienne, I sit up and look around. We appear to be alone. I rub my face, wondering if maybe I'm still asleep. Is this like the last time we had a shared vision?

And then... the ground underneath us rumbles.

Vienne jerks awake. She rises to her knees as her eyes dart about, taking in where we are.

We got out? she asks, mystified. *How?*

I shake my head. I have a feeling that what we're seeing right now isn't entirely real.

The rumbling continues, and then, on the horizon, I make out an immense shape. It rears up into the sky, blotting out the moon. The creature is long and cylindrical, but massive, almost beyond comprehension.

Then, we hear panicked voices. Suddenly, over the top of the hill come more figures. They're all humanoid in shape, and they're rushing straight toward us.

I grab Vienne and pull her to her feet, both of us naked. In the faint light of the moon I can just barely make them out: humans and trollkin, their feet pounding the ground as they head down the hillside. They rush past us, as if we aren't there, dressed in leathers and shouting at one another in a language I can't understand.

Suddenly, a horrible screech tears through the air. The massive creature on the horizon slams down into the ground, causing everything to shake.

It's one of the great worms, Vienne says, gaping in awe. *That's what that is!*

Creatures from legend that once roamed the earth, right here in front of us. Where are we? What have we appeared in the middle of?

That's when I realize the worm is *moving,* and it's moving fast. It plows through the ground, clearly heading toward us. Dirt flies into the air as it devours the earth underneath it.

Oh, fuck. Vienne grabs me and begins running. Though my eyes are riveted on the beast bee-lining toward us, I manage to make my feet move, too.

Vienne drags me down the hill, out of the huge beast's path, but I don't know if we'll make it far enough in time. The creature is bearing down on us, almost bigger than the mountain itself. Its huge, wide mouth is gaping as it devours the ground.

Run, Graz! Run! But even as she urges me on, her short legs are causing her to fall behind me. Without a second thought, I haul Vienne into my arms, then race forward as fast as my legs possibly can. I will get her and my whelp to safety, even if it costs me everything.

Right as the gaping mouth of the monstrous beast is about to suck us into its vortex, I hurl both of us out of the way. We tumble to the ground, and I hold Vienne tight in the protective circle of my arms as I roll over rocks and dirt down the hillside.

The terrible worm shoots past us, hurling dust into the air. We cover our heads as clods of dirt rain down, the wrinkled skin of the monster blowing by.

We hear screams up ahead. I wonder how many of the others were able to get out of the way? I don't release Vienne until the gargantuan worm's tail tip finally slides out of sight, over the curve of the hill.

Graz! She turns to me with fire in her eyes. *It's the myth. The story!*

What story?

She just shakes her head like it will take too long to explain. *Follow me.*

Without another look, Vienne takes off running in her bare feet along the canyon the worm has left in its wake. All I can do is chase behind her. I know she wouldn't stop even if I begged her.

We're both panting and worn out as we crest the hill—but then another catastrophic shriek shakes the air. Up ahead, the worm has stopped its advance and now, is reared up high into the air, taller than the tallest peak. But there's a huge blotch of red on it, blood pouring down the long body.

Then, a bright beam of purple light shoots from the ground and into the sky, striking the monster again. More blood spurts out, and it howls with pain. The worm whips back, and Vienne nods at me.

Keep going. She sprints down the hillside, toward the fight.

Vienne! I call after her, trailing in her footsteps as we near the battle.

More bursts of light. The creature's mouth opens wide and black slime gushes out.

There! Vienne skids to a halt. *Look!*

Down below, I can make out two figures—a human woman with thick black hair, and a blue troll beside her with a red mane. They stand close together, with one arm around each other, their other hands pointed up at the sky.

Another beam of purple light shoots from their

outstretched palms, striking the worm again. This time, it goes right through the beast, emerging on the other side and blasting up into the sky, where it vanishes.

The force of the beast's cry shakes the earth. This last blow has made an impact. That's when the worm falls.

Its whole body twists in the air, and when it lands, striking the earth, the entire ground shakes. Both Vienne and I lose our footholds, and I barely catch her before she falls over. More black muck spills from the worm's cavernous mouth, and it whines as it writhes.

But soon, its movements slow down. It's dying, that much is clear. Eventually, its breathing ceases, and the gaping mouth gives way, crashing in on itself.

The air falls still. It's as if every living thing in the world is holding its breath, wondering if this is truly the end.

Slowly, the skin on the great worm sags, sticking on its many rib bones like a tent collapsing over the poles. Then the skin crumbles, as if it has suddenly become dust. The bones, too begin to break apart, dissolving into the air like sand.

High up above, the dust from the body is rising, swirling into a small tornado. We all cover our faces to hide from the debris as the tornado whips faster and faster, spiraling up into the air. A bright speck of light appears at the top, and a booming voice fills the valley.

"*You believe you have defeated me.*" A terrible laugh echoes off the mountaintops. "*Foolish mortals. I will become one of you. I will use you to destroy yourselves.*"

And with that, the blip of light shoots off into the sky. It arcs high up, then down again over on the other side of the mountains before vanishing.

The dust falls to the ground, scattering everywhere. No other remnants of the worm remain.

CHAPTER 22

*W*hat in the fuck just happened?

We stand on the hillside, both of us gaping at the place where the behemoth used to be. Far below us, the pair of warriors who took it down lower their hands, and the woman collapses in the troll's arms.

Suddenly, the world in front of me swims. Everything turns blurry, and I feel my legs give out from under me. Then my vision goes black.

Just as abruptly as I passed out, I wake again. I sit up, squinting against the bright glow of purple magic in the otherwise dark room. Graz is beside me, groaning as he opens his eyes. The mattress must have disappeared while we were asleep and now we're lying on the hard stone floor. I quickly grab my clothes and pull them on so I'm not so cold.

What was that? Graz asks as he rolls over, squinting at me. *You were there, too.*

It was another one of those visions. I try to remember every-thing that happened before we fell asleep. I tried to use magic to get out of our tomb, but nothing happened.

Perhaps the vision was its response to us. Maybe, to escape this place, we need to be like that troll and that human we saw.

The legend of Riggamora, I say thoughtfully. It's clear to me that what we saw was the same moment as the illustration in the book: when trollkin and humans worked together to destroy the last great worm, the greatest of them all. *That's what that was. The end of Riggamora.*

But he didn't disappear, like the book said. In our vision, he survived the obliteration of his body. He *lived,* though only in spirit. He threatened to obtain a mortal form, and then...

The legend of what? Graz asks, also gathering up his clothes.

It's a very old story. We saw carvings of it, too, in the last ruin.

He strokes his chin. *You're right. But... why did we see that? We know why we saw the last one.* His arm snakes around my waist, pulling me across the floor until I'm against his side. *But why this one?*

I think the magic is trying to show us something. It is odd, to think of it like that—as its own entity, perhaps with its own thoughts and intentions. *We got the wish we made. We just didn't get it how we expected.*

So, what, we blast a beam of magic together through the ceiling? Graz asks skeptically.

I think for a few long moments. We can't force our way out, or we risk collapsing the whole place with us inside it. But maybe it's simpler than that.

I stand up and observe the carvings on the wall around us. They are standard fare now, lots of faces staring into one another's eyes in human-trollkin pairs. There are so many of them, though, not just one. My brow furrows as I trace the progression around the room.

I think... I'm hesitant to say the words, because it's just a guess. *I think that once upon a time, there were many couples like us.*

Graz lifts his head, listening.

Remember what Riggamora said? 'I will use you to destroy yourselves.' He was right. Once upon a time, we got along. But somehow, between then and now, our civilizations have done nothing but fight.

He nods. *As long as our written record has existed.*

But it wasn't always that way. I think Riggamora has done what he promised.

I can't explain it, but why else would our civilizations have forgotten how we once lived side-by-side? I look down into the glowing pool, baffled by its existence. Graz peers over my shoulder.

Perhaps he's still out there. Right now.

I shudder at the thought, but it's possible. Is it also possible that all this war, all this death, is because of one entity?

He was defeated once. I reach up and clasp Graz's hand in mine. *Together, that woman and that troll took him down.*

Together, and with the help of magic.

I reach into the pool, lifting out a handful of the glowing purple substance. Graz extends his palm, too, cupping it underneath mine. In our hands, the magic glows brighter, then brighter still.

What if we made a wish together? Graz says, his front to my back so I can feel all of him. *Is that what it's trying to tell us?*

Maybe he's right, and the key to all of this is that we have to work as one, the same way those two in the vision did.

All right. No harm in trying. *What should we wish for?*

Freedom? Graz suggests.

I nod. *Straightforward enough.*

I close my eyes and lean back, and we hold out our hands

together. I imprint my desire as clearly as possible. *Let us be free.*

The magic glows even brighter, blinding me. Then it bursts, showering us in purple sparks.

Overhead, the stone rumbles as it begins to move.

Graz

I hold onto Vienne as our rock tomb shakes under our feet. Then, our escape passage is revealed again.

Ladder. I quickly scoop up some more magic and wish for what I need. Overhead, a familiar face appears.

"You're alive!" Gusak says with surprise.

"We're coming out." I set the ladder against the wall, and I climb up first so I can protect Vienne, whatever Gusak decides to do to her. I hope he won't try to punish her for earlier, because I won't stand for it, and I don't want to face off against my boss.

When I get to the top, I help Vienne climb the rest of the way up, and I wrap an arm around her. Agna has her weapon in hand, already aiming it. Vienne reaches for her gun, but I stop her.

We don't need to fight, I tell her firmly. She shoots each of the other trollkin in the room a deadly glare, but releases the gun she took from Kal'zan. He doesn't look pleased about it, but he doesn't attempt to get it back, either.

"What did you find down there?" Gusak asks me. He quirks a brow at Vienne. "You two were rather loud."

Ugh, he heard all that?

"The legends about magic are true," is all I can say by way of explanation. "It's a long story."

Gusak takes one last look over the edge, at the pool of magic far below, and I hope we aren't going to come to conflict over it. I would be forced to defend what's mine.

"Do we have to worry about your mate blowing up the mountain?" Gusak asks, sarcasm in his voice. He shoots Vienne a scathing look.

Do you still want it destroyed? I ask, peering down at her. *It is dangerous, you're right. But it's also—*

I can see the value, Vienne interrupts. *Now that we know Riggamora is still out in the world, what if he has to be defeated again?*

I nod slowly. *There is always that possibility. Though we may not be the ones to do it.*

Vienne sighs. *This isn't what I came here to do,* she says sadly. *But I think Mom will understand. Who knows if we'll need that power again someday.*

I nod in agreement.

Let's seal it, she says. *Lock it away, so no one can stumble across it by accident.*

That's what we'll be: the guardians of this power. We'll hide it until it's needed again, if we can get Gusak to agree.

I flash her a smile as I pull her into my arms. *My wise woman,* I say, resting my forehead against hers.

"All right, all right," Gusak says with an impatient groan.

"We're leaving it here." I give him a firm look, daring him to challenge me. "We're going to seal it away, so no one can stumble across it."

Gusak scowls. "That wasn't in my plan, bookworm."

"I don't care what was in your plan. Are you going to shoot us to get what you want?" I pull Vienne closer, ready to put myself between the two of them. "Magic wasn't meant for you. It was meant to protect us—all of us—should we need it."

Gusak studies me for a long, silent moment, then rocks back on his heels.

"We should get out of here," he says to Agna and Kal'zan. "We don't want to risk direct exposure and get sick, too."

They both nod in agreement, and head out the tunnel the way we came in, leaving Vienne and I standing over the chasm in the floor. I sigh with relief, glad that it won't come to blows with my boss.

We're clear, I tell Vienne. With a nod, she finds her pack and reaches in, withdrawing a water skin. When she opens the lid, bright purple light streams out.

You've had that with you the whole time? I ask, marveling. *No wonder your boss got as sick as he did.*

She glances down at it. *Oh. Really?* A smirk crosses her face as she spills some into her hand. I hold mine out, too, and she pours me a few drops. We hold our hands together.

Seal this place away, she says, and we both tip our palms to spill it onto the ground. *Only allow in others like us, who seek this power to protect the world from future threats.*

Both droplets hit the stone floor with a sizzle, then vanish.

We had better go, I tell her. As if to emphasize my point, the stone all around us begins shaking.

We rush together to the tunnel that will lead us out. I hope the mountain will give us a moment to escape before it does whatever it's going to do.

Finally, we're in the fresh air again. There, Gusak, Agna and Kal'zan stand on the ledge, but all of them have their hands raised in the air.

"What's going on?" I ask as we emerge.

Gusak shakes his head. "You're a little late."

VIENNE

Fuck. It's Raiden.

I thought I could shake him off like a flea, but here he is again—and he's the one with the gun. His arm is shaking wildly, and if he decided to let off a shot, who knows who or what he'd hit with it?

The mountain is rumbling, and now, smoke pours out of the top. It's a volcano, just like I thought. And it's going to blow. We have to get out of here, and fast.

I don't think, I just do.

I lunge at Raiden, and he instantly fires his weapon. The bullet strikes me in the thigh, spattering blood. Pain blows through my body, but it's too late.

Vienne! Graz heads toward me, but I need to keep him safe. I need to keep him away from Raiden. I slam into my idiot ex with my shoulder aimed at his diaphragm, and instantly, he crumples forward.

"Bitch!" Raiden shouts, shooting his gun again, but this time the bullet hits the stone cliff face next to us. He stumbles back, closer to the edge of the staircase.

"Yep," I answer, struggling to keep standing on my injured leg.

So once more, I throw my weight into the bastard, and he finally loses his footing. He reaches toward me with one hand, probably hoping to grab onto me and prevent what's about to happen, but I manage to stumble back out of the way.

He grasps at air, and with nothing to keep him from falling, he topples backward right off the steps.

Raiden screams as he falls. Graz catches me before I can slip down the stairs to my own death, holding me firm in his arms as Raiden disappears. His tortured howl fills the air, but then it fades.

We don't even hear him hit the bottom.

Gasping, I finally collapse, the pain in my thigh too much to bear. Graz crouches over me, his expression beyond worry.

Fuck, your leg, he says, examining my wound with horror. *You're bleeding everywhere.*

But the mountain is still rumbling, the smoke pouring out of the top growing thicker and thicker around us.

We have to go. Now! I manage to get to my feet, even though putting any pressure at all on my leg fills my whole body with flaming agony. Graz wraps his arm around me, and suddenly, the other big orc—Gusak—appears on my other side. He slings my arm over his shoulder, and the two of them manage to take the weight off my leg.

Together, we move down the steps as fast as we can. The big troll leads the way, the orc woman bringing up the rear as we navigate our way down, all while the mountain shakes under our feet.

That's when I look up, and see the lava starting to pour down the side.

Go! I tell Graz. *Go, go!*

All of us hurry our pace, though I know I'm slowing everyone down. We don't even have time to try to use magic to help us. All we can do is run.

Ledge after ledge, we race the slowly flowing lava down the mountainside. Belatedly, I think maybe we should have waited until we got out safely to seal this place off.

Too late now.

Then, at last, we reach the bottom. We made it. We're going to live, if we can just get away from this volcano fast enough. But we won't get very far if Gusak and Graz have to carry me the entire way.

I make them set me down, then gesture at my pack. *Graz— the magic. Get it out.*

Obediently, Graz pulls the water skin out of my pack, opens the lid, and pours some of the purple fluid into his hand. Gusak takes a cautious step back as Graz closes his eyes, then tilts his palm, dripping the magic onto my thigh.

At first, nothing happens, and I wonder if perhaps we've reached the limit of what it can do. Then, suddenly, my whole body is filled with burning, excruciating pain.

I cry out, crumpling forward to protect my wound.

Fuck, what did I do? Graz holds me as I moan.

My very flesh starts moving under my hands, and I wonder what Graz has done. Oh, it hurts worse than anything I've ever experienced. The wound seizes, and then suddenly...

The bullet is ejected. It shoots out of my thigh, covered in blood, and tumbles off the edge of the cliffside. Then the flesh starts to bind together again, until all that's left is a reddened patch of scarred skin.

We both stare at it, and then at each other. The other trollkin let out sounds of awe and appreciation, while Graz smiles.

Amazing, he says, helping me up to my feet. The pain is gone now, but we still have a long way to go before we're safe.

CHAPTER 23

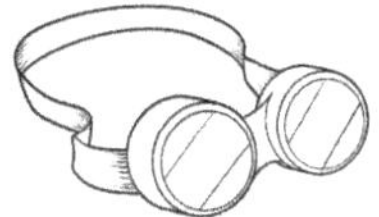

GRAZ

Now that Vienne can get around on her leg again, we sprint down the hill as fast as we can while hot lava finally reaches the base of the mountain. It flows toward us, but it's slow enough we're making good progress getting ahead of it. I remember that less than a mile away, there's a river with a bridge crossing. If we can make it to the other side, the river should slow the lava down.

We're all panting by the time we reach where we'd left the horses tied up this morning, and we hurriedly pack up and untie them. I toss Vienne onto one horse's back because her legs are shorter than mine, and this way, she can keep up.

Then we're off again as another massive plume of smoke is belched into the air. The mountain itself is shaking, and Gusak gives it a skeptical look over his shoulder.

"I think this is about to get a lot worse," he says. And sure enough, right then, a massive fountain of lava shoots out the top, scattering across the hillsides.

"Run!" I urge Vienne's horse on ahead, and start running myself.

We all push ourselves as hard as we can as the peak erupts. Smoke and ash fills the sky, and I wonder if we've done something even worse than destroying that pool of magic.

But the lava never reaches us. Soon, the shaking under our feet slows, and behind us, the lava has reached the river. Sure enough, it doesn't spread past the water, and far behind us, the peak starts to cool.

At last, it seems we're out of range of the eruption. I come to a stop, sweating profusely and gasping for air. Gusak climbs off his horse, peering up at the darkened sky.

"What in the hell did you two do?"

I sigh, not looking forward to explaining the choice we made. I reach up to Vienne on the horse, clasping her hand in mine.

"We locked it away." I grimace. "Now no one can get to it."

Gusak is agog. "You made a fucking *volcano* erupt." He shakes his head ruefully. "I came all this way for that?"

What now? Vienne asks, squeezing my fingers in return. *I ought to go back and tell my mom what happened. She'll want to know the legend was true.*

Which means separating, as I can't follow her home to the human capital city—and I don't know where I stand with Gusak, either.

"Are you going to keep us prisoner?" I ask him.

He rubs his chin. "I ought to. I certainly shouldn't let her go." He nods at Vienne, who glares at him in return. Agna takes out her weapon, and Vienne drops her hand to her own gun—well, the one she stole from Kal'zan, anyway.

Gusak sighs and holds up his hands. "All right, everyone calm down." He glares at me. "Tell your woman to relax."

I could laugh in his face. "She's not going to. Not while she has our whelp to protect."

His eyebrow jumps. "Oh? Is that so?"

Vienne is clearly annoyed that we're having a conversation without her. *What's going on? What's he saying?*

He's trying to decide what to do with us, I explain.

What to do with us?! She drops her hand to her gun. *He doesn't get to decide that!*

Damn it, how am I going to get her out of this situation safely?

"And what do *you* intend to do?" Gusak asks, squaring his shoulders. "Where do you think you and your little human mate will be safe with said whelp? You ought to return to Kalishagg. Stay under my protection."

Vienne will never accept an outcome like that, even if it's rather magnanimous of my boss to suggest it. She would never live under someone else's thumb.

"You still work for me," Gusak tells me in a warning tone. "Those are the terms for keeping your little human as your pet."

Vienne still has her hand on her gun, and so does Agna. This is not looking good for anyone.

"What if I still work for you?" I ask hastily, putting myself between Vienne and Gusak. "You can have my shop. We could go to Eyra Cove—we've heard there are others like us there— and I could be a go-between for you. I know it's the next neutral city in your sights."

Gusak arches an eyebrow. "You would get me a foothold in Eyra Cove?"

I nod rapidly. "And I could make contact with Lo'zar. He has connections to the human underworld."

This seems to get through. Gusak taps his chin, thinking, as we all wait with bated breath.

What's he deciding? Vienne asks cautiously.

We might get to leave if I work for him.

She scowls. *For this criminal?*

All I can do is nod while I wait for Gusak to make his decision. He studies me like I'm an insect he's about to crush under one shoe.

"Fine." Gusak nods at Agna, who stands down. "I have one additional condition, though."

I know I don't have a choice, so I ask, "What is it?"

He gestures at Vienne. "The magic. I want some, in a container like yours that makes it safe."

I squint at him. This feels like a very, very bad idea—but if it means that Vienne and I can get away safely...

I suppose I have to do it. What's the most damage he could possibly do with a few drops of magic?

"All right," I say with a deep sigh. "I'll do it."

Vienne shoots me an annoyed look. *What are you agreeing to?*

To give him a little magic. I'll have to go back to my shop to—

You can't be serious! She looks ready to hop off the horse and strangle me. *You're going to hand some over to some mob boss?*

I walk over to the horse and take her hand in mine. *This is what we have to do if we want to get out of this.*

She studies me skeptically, but I can tell she's weighing the benefits. We get out of here alive, on one side, or we become Gusak's prisoners.

But you can't give it to him as it is, Vienne finally says, eyes narrowed. *Can you stop him from doing anything dangerous with it?*

I hadn't considered that. I could imprint the magic with my own desire before sealing it up, and do it without Gusak being any the wiser.

I grin up at my mate, impressed with her yet again.

Good idea.

Then I'll accept, she says, straightening on the horse and leaving her gun where it is in her holster.

"We'll do it," I tell Gusak, and he clucks in approval.

"Then let's get the fuck out of here," Kal'zan interjects. "Before we run into humans."

Vienne keeps his gun, and no one tries to fight her for it.

Vienne

We have no choice but to go separate ways—for now. Graz has a job to do for his boss before he can be free, and I have a lot to tell Mom. And it'll be much easier traveling by myself in human territory.

I'll be glad to never see that big orc Gusak or his two cronies again, that's for sure.

But we have a plan and a destination: the neutral city of Eyra Cove, far off the coast in the Frattern Islands. The whole area is contested territory, so even though we live in times of peace, it can be a dicey place to go.

Still, there are others there, like Graz and I. Like our child will be. It's as good of a place as any to put down roots. Not that we'll live that way for the long term, but it sure would be nice to slow down for a while after all this.

How I'm going to explain what happened to Raiden, though... I hope I can get in and out of Culberra before anyone starts to inquire about the night I left and shot a hole through my ceiling.

Carting around magic the way I have been is dangerous, we both know, so Graz and I decide to dispose of it. Then he pulls me into his arms and buries his face in my hair.

I'll see you really soon. He runs a hand down over my belly. *Both of you. All right?*

You don't need to assure me. I rub one of his tusks affectionately. *If you don't show up, I'll hunt you down.*

He snickers. *I know you will.*

It's hard watching him go, but it's the right thing for now.

As soon as I make it back to Culberra, I head right to find Mom. I'm simply buzzing with how much I have to tell her, but weighed down that I'll have to say goodbye, too. She won't leave the archive, as afraid of the outside world as she is, and I don't know how often I'll be able to come and see her once I have the baby.

When she finally lets me in, Mom pulls me into her arms and hugs me tight, which isn't the usual greeting for her.

"I'm so glad you're all right," she murmurs. "When you didn't come back, I was so worried! It looked like your apartment had been ransacked."

I sigh. "It was."

"By who?"

"Sit down and pour yourself some wine," I tell her. "Have I got the story you won't believe."

Not to mention that she's going to be a grandmother.

My mother listens raptly as I spill everything, from reuniting with Graz to the damned kingpin he brought along with him. What we saw in our vision, what choice we decided to make.

"It was all true, just like you said." I lean back in my chair. "But Riggamora isn't gone."

"I wonder where he is now. If all of this war and death in my lifetime was his doing, somehow." Mom leans across the desk toward me. "I think you made the right choice. And going to Eyra Cove—where you can be with others like you—is the right choice, too." She sighs. "My daughter. Always so damned smart."

I laugh, because her approval means the world to me.

"Never expected you'd be having a child of your own, though," she says thoughtfully. "Certainly not with an orc."

She's taking this all much better than I expected. I'm so grateful for her, I hug her once more. Then she snaps her fingers in the air.

"I got most of your things." Mom urges me to follow her into the back of the archives. "You shouldn't go back to your apartment. I think it's being watched. Raiden must have told someone where he was going."

Fuck. Does that make me an outlaw? Well, I guess this makes packing simpler.

I rifle through what she was able to recover from my home for what's most important, then load up two bags. Then Mom suggests I get going now, just in case anyone's seen me.

She hugs me again, her eyes soft. "I'll come," she says. "Send me a letter when you have the baby, and I'll come visit."

I gape at her. "Really? You'll leave the archive?"

"To see my grandchild? Of course." She kisses my cheek. "Now go. You don't want to leave your new husband waiting."

I groan. "That's not... ugh. Never mind." I kiss her back, and then I'm off to find my new life across the sea.

CHAPTER 24

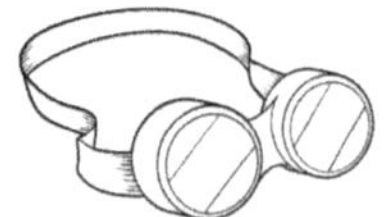

I am absolutely done with riding horses, I can tell you that. I just want to sleep in a soft bed and have my mate with me again. But I know, even once we make it back to Kalishagg, that it's still weeks, if not months away. I want to be there with her during this, but who knows how long Gusak will keep me around to wrap things up before I can go to Eyra Cove?

Unfortunately, it doesn't look like I'll be able to get rid of him anytime soon. But I've already sent off a note to Lo'zar, charmed with a drop of magic to travel the world to wherever he's found himself, and warn him we're coming—with the caveat that he should stay on the lookout for Gusak. I don't know if the boss is really willing to give him a pardon or simply waiting for the right moment to strike.

But I wouldn't mind having my best friend at my side when my whelp comes.

I make quick work of devising another container for Gusak, something he can keep close to him. I find an old pocketwatch casing and make some alterations, then pour in a few drops of magic before imprinting my wish on it and sealing it away, just as Vienne and I discussed.

I'm ashamed to admit that I keep the rest, stuffing the box away deep down in my pack. Then I sell Jaks at the stables, and break down Izzy's cage into panels I can take with me. He's coming along whether Vienne likes it or not. At least he seems to have returned to being his old self again. And selling Jaks once and for all pads my wallet nicely.

Kugara confesses to turning me in to the boss, which shouldn't surprise me, but it certainly helps me feel less guilty about leaving her behind.

Gusak is surprisingly merciful once I hand over the watch. After looking it over carefully, he nods in approval and slips it into his pocket.

"Now go live your life, bookworm," he says with a snort, slapping me on the back—*hard*. I choke a little as I stumble forward. "I hear there's a boat leaving in not too long. Maybe you should be on it."

I can't tell if it's a threat or an encouragement. Either way, the second he says I'm free to go, I'm hauling ass with my bags and my lizard for that ship.

Ugh, it's too bad we had to choose an island, though. We'll have to cross the sea anytime we want to come or go, and my stomach doesn't like the sound of that. Izzy, too, seems displeased with the constant rocking of the boat.

I can't wait to be on dry land again, and see Vienne with my own eyes instead of just in my dreams.

After ages on that goddamned boat, we finally arrive at the Frattern Islands: little more than windswept cliffs that overlook a choppy sea. But as we approach the harbor, the swarm of activity that is Eyra Cove is obvious. Many other ships are anchored there, awaiting passengers coming and going. Ramps lead up from one platform to the next, connecting all the different levels of the city. It looks precarious to me.

This is my new home, though, so I'd better get used to it.

Foolishly, we didn't make any arrangements as to how we'd find one another, both of us thinking it would be a smaller city. Irritated, I drag my bags off the ship along with Izzy, and make my way through town searching for some kind of inn. I have enough coin to stay for a time, and hopefully find somewhere we can live more permanently.

It's shocking to see so many humans and trollkin alike bustling about Eyra Cove, all mixed up together. Though the winds are sharp, the sun is shining, and I'm surprised to find myself filled with... hope. An excitement for what the future holds.

Once I'm settled in with Izzy in his cage once more, I stuff my hands in my pockets and go searching. I still have my box with me should I truly struggle to find Vienne, but I have a feeling that I'll see my mate again when the time is right.

Fate has played many games with us. What's one more?

I stop a few places along the way to grab a bite to eat and admire some of the artisanal goods on sale. It looks like respectable craftsmen from all over gather here, and I find many serious warriors and other freelancers carefully inspecting the gear before they buy.

That's when something truly massive catches my eye. It's not an orc or a troll, towering above the crowd.

It's an ogre.

I blink a few more times, wondering if what I'm seeing is

just an optical illusion. But when he steps into view, all of him, I know I'm right.

I thought ogres had all gone extinct, and yet here's one walking among us like he belongs here, and next to him...

A human. She's rather small, with gratuitous dark hair tumbling down her back, and her hand is clasped tightly in his. They're smiling at one another, the mutual affection clear in their faces.

I know my cue when I see it.

VIENNE

I feel like I've been waiting forever. I'm still not showing yet, but it's tiring searching the city every day for my wayward inventor. Too much walking makes me sleepy, and the different smells all make me want to vomit.

I hope Gusak didn't change his mind and decide to keep Graz captive after all.

Taking up a room at the inn, I start asking around about my taboo topic: humans and trollkin couples. Finally, I'm directed to the leatherworker's shop.

"That's where you'll find the weirdos," the barkeep says, rolling his eyes. "They caused me a whole mess, you know."

I don't know what he means by that, but I follow the instructions anyway down the gangway to a row of shops. The leatherworker's has a nice storefront with lots of high-quality boots, gloves, and armor on display, perfect for anyone trying to repel an arrow or simply look fashionable. I'm eyeballing a pair of fur-rimmed boots when a bright and eager red-headed woman comes to the counter.

"See something you like?" she asks. Beside me, a human

man starts leafing through the goods. I catch him trying to steal a buckle from the corner of my eye, but before I can move or speak, a huge, blue troll approaches the man from behind.

"Put. Down." The troll's accent is thick, but his words are clear. The man freezes, then drops the buckle and backs away. The troll crosses his arms and watches as the human quickly makes himself scarce.

The red-headed woman isn't surprised in the least, though. She rolls her eyes and says, "Raz'jin, *gurak ag sar.*"

I stare at her. She can speak Trollkin? The troll answers with something that's clearly in jest. Then he hops over the counter, right in front of me, and sweeps the woman up into his arms.

"Oh!" I cry out, and the two of them turn abruptly to look at me. The troll frowns, closing his grip protectively around the woman, who must be his mate. "I'm sorry, I didn't mean to surprise you. You just surprised me. I've been looking for you!"

The woman gives me a funny look. "Us?"

"Well, yes, sort of." I wring my hands together. "Looking for a pair. Like you."

The woman's eyebrows go up, and then she nods vehemently. "You found us. There are others here, too. Are you...?" She trails off.

I grin. "Yes. He's on his way."

The woman looks simply gleeful. "Well, are you looking for a place to stay? We have some friends with a little more room."

And that's how I meet Telise and Raz'jin, the fiery, red-headed woman and her troll mate, who's just as fiery and just as red-headed. They have a son, too, who appears to be one hundred percent troll.

"That's just how it happens," Telise explains. "They come out like one or the other."

The proof is in the pudding. When I meet Mia and Cragnorr, the ogre-human couple, I understand immediately. They have two daughters: an ogre girl who's already the size of a human teenager, and a younger daughter who's all human. She looks just like her mother, whereas their oldest looks like her father.

It is strange, but beautiful. I wonder how ours will come out.

Mia, a lovely young woman who never stops talking, is happy to put me up at their home. Cragnorr, on the other hand, who's as tall as a house and built like one, too, almost never says a word. I still haven't heard him speak except in grunts, or the one time he had to stop his tiny human daughter from eating a bug she found.

Still, I haven't heard from my orc, and I hope he's all right out there, and that he'll be with me soon. But I know I just have to be patient.

Then one evening, while I'm watching over the two little ones, Mia's loud voice rings out.

"Vienne!" She throws the door open. "Vienne, he's here!"

Graz

Seeing my woman again... there is no greater relief in the world.

I lunge at Vienne the moment I see her, tangling her up in my arms and squeezing her for all she's worth. She laughs, burying her face in my chest as I finally set her back on the ground. Then I lean back so I can get a good look at her, and her sky-blue eyes are glittering bright.

Graz, she says, the relief in her voice palpable. *You made it.*

Of course I made it. I gesture to Cragnorr, the huge ogre who stands a few paces behind me. *How could I miss this guy?*

Mia and Cragnorr understand right away that Vienne and I could use a moment together to collect ourselves, so they gather up their children and head off into town to do some shopping.

The moment we're inside the room they've lent Vienne and the door is closed behind me, I'm on top of her, pushing her down to the bed and then crushing her mouth with mine. My sweet mate curls her legs around my waist, pulling me in tighter against her.

Witnessing her with my own eyes again is a gift. Her belly is slightly curved, so only I would notice. I'm only sorry that she's had to go through so much of her pregnancy alone already, but the future will be ours.

I'm so glad you're here, she says while she kisses me harder. One of the advantages to speaking inside your mind is that you can do it while you're plundering your mate's mouth. *I'm so glad you made it.*

I wouldn't miss it for the world. I pull away long enough to examine her flawless body. *How are you? How is the whelp?*

We're fine. She takes one of my hands and guides it down between us, resting it on her belly. *Not much happening yet, but soon, I'm sure.*

I'm awash with the joy of knowing she's safe and sound. And even better, she's discovered what we were looking for—a community where we might be able to belong.

It isn't long before I have all of Vienne's clothes peeled off, and she's lying naked in front of me, her perfect cunt hidden by her brownish-blonde curls. I test every part of her body with my mouth, sampling her throat, her sweat, her nipples. Then I pull her strong thighs apart and attack her between them, drinking her up like the most delicate nectar, playing with her until she's writhing and bucking. I squeeze my fingers inside her, stroking her and winding her up wilder and wilder until she's perfectly ready for my cock.

But she has matters to attend to, as well. Before I can fuck her, she falls to her knees in front of me and takes me between her lips. I nearly buckle forward at the sensation of her wet tongue.

You taste so good, she murmurs, licking me up before sinking me into her throat. My eyes roll back in my head and my balls tighten as she pleasures me with her mouth.

Wait, wait. I'm gasping, holding onto her shoulders so I don't let go too soon. *I need to be inside you.*

Vienne grins around my thick cock and releases it, then climbs back onto the bed. She spreads her legs, touching herself with a wicked look.

Fuck. I can't hold off a moment longer.

I'm going to stuff that cunt so full of me, I growl as I climb on top of her, grabbing both her wrists in my hand and pinning them above her head. My woman's hips rise up to mine as she demands me with her body.

I guide my cock through the pink, swollen lips of her cunt, gritting my teeth to keep from plunging right into her.

Oh, you're so tight, I mutter as I push into her, watching her petals unfurl for me. How such a small body can take mine is a mystery. Vienne moans as I thrust shallowly, trying to get her used to me once more.

And then, I sink into her. What bliss it is, to be together again. My mate's silky depths welcome me in, swallowing my cock until I can't fit any more of it inside her. Then, slowly, I make love to her, devouring each of her moans and cries, finally feeling at peace as our souls come to rest next to each other once again.

The harder I fuck her, the more she screams something unintelligible, and I bury myself as deep as I can before I let it all go. Vienne pulses around me, squeezing me, drawing every last drop of my seed from my cock that she can.

Then I roll her up in my arms and collapse to the bed, finally back where I belong.

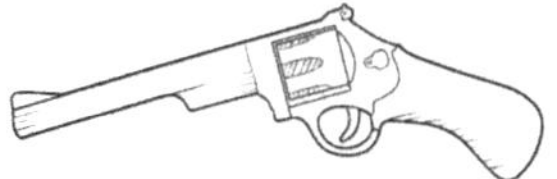

VIENNE

We do manage to find our own home, in a back alleyway above a pawn shop with enough room for the baby and Izzy, too. That lizard has grown on me, and he's even taken to laying around on my lap from time to time.

I expected more resistance from the owner to let us rent, given that we're one human and one orc, but the woman seemed more annoyed than anything that we were taking up her time. We agreed to her price, and she surveyed each of us.

"I hope you work," she said. "Your rent will be due at the beginning of every month, on the dot."

"Right." I bite the inside of my cheek, hoping I do manage to find something before then.

When she's gone, Graz pats my arm. *Don't worry. Lo'zar will find us soon, and I have work I can do for Gusak.*

We wait for this mysterious friend of his to appear. Some of my sickness eases, to be replaced by other annoying symptoms —aches and pains, sleeplessness.

Did you really have to put a baby in me? I grumble as we spoon in bed, Graz's hand exploring me all over.

Sorry. But he doesn't seem sorry as he winds his hand down between my legs, teasing me and tantalizing me until I'm ready for him. We start on our sides, but soon Graz insists on seeing my belly while he fucks me, positioning me on his lap so he can suck my nipples while I ride him.

Ah, filled up with my whelp, are you? he says, bringing me down on his cock until I'm whining and clutching him close.

Yes! I can barely think when he takes me like this. *I'm so full with you!*

Graz grunts with pleasure as he sinks deep inside me, rocking back and forth there as he touches me all over. He takes me like that until I'm muttering incoherently, then pushes me down and fucks me until I gush around him.

I'm starting to get rather round when there comes an unexpected knock at our door.

Hmm, an unfamiliar voice says. *I thought this was the place.*

You just knocked. Let's wait a minute.

It must be them. Who else can speak the way that Graz and I can?

Graz throws open the door, and standing on the other side is a very tall, lanky troll with purple skin and even purpler hair, and beside him is a tiny woman with black hair and huge eyes. A little human toddler stands at her side, holding her hand, and another is slung over the troll's shoulders.

"Ah!" the troll calls out. "Graz!"

I understand this, at least. The other woman and I both scoot aside so the two can hug in the doorway, then they start throwing words back and forth in Trollkin we can't understand.

I hate when you do that, the woman with the dark hair says, frowning at her mate, who must be Lo'zar. *What are you saying?*

I have to laugh. *We can understand you, too,* I say.

The troll's eyes jump to mine, and his mouth widens into an impossibly charming grin. *Ah, the woman who broke my grumpy best friend.* He walks over to me and grabs me by the shoulder. *I knew he'd eat his words one day.*

We welcome them all inside, and it's sweet to see Graz and his old friend reunited. Rimi, Lo'zar's mate, isn't as talkative as Lo'zar is. She studies everyone as her twin toddlers sit meekly beside her.

"Two of them, huh?" I ask as our mates talk.

"Oof, they were a task, I'll tell you what," she says. "You're sure you have just one on the way?"

I laugh. "I think it's just one."

It's a delight to get to know her and hear her story, which is almost as wild as ours. We share what we know about magic, and it's a relief to find someone else who's been there, who's witnessed it and what it can do.

"I think you made the right choice to seal it off," she says thoughtfully. "Who knows when Riggamora will show his face again?" She pats one of her children on the head, and I wonder if she knows something I don't.

GRAZ

Lo'zar couldn't believe his ears when I told him that he might finally be safe from Gusak.

"I mean, don't use me as a reference or anything," I say

quickly. "But it seemed like he understood where you were coming from."

My friend settles his little human son in his lap as he leans back in a chair, one of the two we have on our new wooden porch.

"I hope so. I'd love to get to be landside, just for a while. I think the twins could use some hard ground under their feet."

I nod in understanding. They're easygoing children, as far as children go, but there's something to be said for stability.

"I'm so happy you found what you needed," Lo'zar says, clapping me on the shoulder. "And you got out from under the clan."

"Gusak still has his claws in me." I grit my teeth. "But I have to do what I have to do for my whelp."

Lo'zar just laughs, and I hate how everything is a joke of some sort to him. "He can't do shit to you here. Gusak makes you think the whole world is his, that he can hurt you wherever he finds you, but his claws don't extend all that far. Just feed him a little information so he feels relevant and he'll be happy."

I wish I had my friend's carefree attitude.

"Besides, it seems like everyone here protects each other." Lo'zar lifts his drink, toasting the city from the balcony as the sun sets. "I can't believe there are so many of us."

"I can." I remember the last chamber we found, with many, many couples carved into the walls around us. "Once upon a time, I don't think we were that rare."

"Maybe even more will crop up as time goes on and find their way here." He raises his arms high over his head as he yawns. "Would be nice to be a part of the welcoming committee."

"Are you really thinking you'll stay?" I ask, trying to keep the hopeful note out of my voice. Perhaps it's been a long time since we were both children trying to survive on the streets, but seeing Lo'zar again... it reminds me of the old days.

"Sure." He leans back in his chair to peer inside the house. *Rimi! Should we stay?*

I think we should stay, she calls back.

Lo'zar nods as if he expected this. "There you have it. We'll stay."

I grin and elbow him in the arm. "You have to get your own spot, though. There's not enough room here for all of you."

He winks. "Don't worry about us. You know me. I always find a way."

Lo'zar and Rimi park their boat at the dock, and stay there until they can find a more permanent place in Eyra Cove. Vienne and I introduce them to the other couples, though we keep some of the more magical elements of our past a secret.

That's one we don't need to share, not unless the future demands it.

As my mate's body changes, I'm more than happy that Rimi can be there to support her. Vienne has a rather unpleasant pregnancy, and her belly grows larger and faster than any of us expected—except Telise, who just shakes her head and sighs.

"Just like Izzek. You're having an orc baby, I know it."

So I keep Vienne close to me at night, and bring her herbal teas when I can. As always, I tinker away, and I build a tool for Telise to make her stitching work faster. She's so amazed by it that she asks if I can make a few more, which I then sell to other craftspeople living in the city.

Encouraged, I try to come up with a few more inventions that might be helpful to her, like a gadget that can scrape her hides, sparing her an immense amount of time and labor. Soon, other shopkeepers are seeking me out to see what I can make easier for them.

Vienne has to spend much of her time in bed, but her eyes are brilliantly mischievous as orders start coming in.

My clever orc, she says, bending over me at my work bench to kiss me on the cheek. Then she pries my goggles off my head and drags me away to bed with her.

There's nothing in the world like my mate on my lap, swallowing my cock deep inside her, her belly full with my whelp and her breasts growing bigger every day.

I think that certainly, this is what happiness looks like.

Vienne

Telise is, unfortunately, correct. Our son is an orc, green all over just like his father, with a smattering of his thick hair. He has incredible lungs, which he wails with the moment he's born.

Nazag. It's an old-fashioned orc name, but I don't mind it. *He should keep that part of his heritage,* I tell Graz. *Even if, for the most part, we build him a new one.*

I'm not in the most wonderful shape after the birth, as hard as it was, but Graz takes over his duties without missing a step. He lets me rest, keeping the baby with him at his desk while he works. But I know what I need, and it's not to be stuck in bed any longer.

Finally, after nearly two months of healer-mandated recovery, I'm cleared for activity again. I almost couldn't take it any longer, and the moment Graz puts the baby down that night, I tackle him onto the bed.

He laughs as I smother him, riding his belly and kissing him. Then he rolls us over so he's on top of me, resting his weight on mine.

Oh, are you ready? he asks, smoothing his hands down my sides. *Is your cunt hungry for my cock?*

I giggle wildly. *Hungry for everything.* I drag his suspenders off his shoulders, then unbutton his pants so I can push them off, too. When that gorgeous cock of his is exposed to me, I lick it all over the way I might a piece of candy, just enjoying him, until Graz is gripping my hair and begging to put it all inside me. He's so ravenous for me that he pushes me down on the bed on my knees, my ass in the air in front of him, and licks me all over before sinking himself inside me.

It's all I can do not to cry out and wake Nazag as my mate fucks me for everything I'm worth. I ball up the blanket and stuff it in my mouth as he makes me hit my peak, over and over, before he finally lets himself break. Then he leaks out of me all over the bed.

When we're lying together side by side, Graz runs his hand down my side in languid strokes.

I know this isn't your last adventure, he says, nuzzling the side of my head and kissing my ear. *What would you like to do next, once he's a little older?*

I smirk. He knows me well.

Didn't Gusak send you a clue he found? Some ruins up in the far north? I ask.

Oh, I suppose he did. I did a very basic inquiry about it, but didn't find much. Graz raises an eyebrow at me. *You think we should go check out the source?*

A smile spreads across my face. *Why not? We can bring the kid along. It'll be good for him.*

Graz chuckles into my hair. *If you insist.*

I fall asleep that way, wrapped tight in my mate's arms, dreaming about what other mysteries we might uncover.

THANK YOU FOR READING!

I hope you enjoyed Graz and Vienne's story. If you liked this book, please consider leaving a review! Reviews help indie authors in finding new readers.

And be sure to check out my other books for even more fun and steamy adventures!

JOIN MY NEWSLETTER!

For all the latest regarding books, and to get a FREE Trollkin Lovers novella, join my newsletter! You can also find signed paperbacks and artwork of your favorite books.

www.LyonneRiley.com

Get even more steamy content by joining my Patreon! I share NSFW artwork of your favorite couples, and even more sexy stories.

Patreon.com/LyonneRiley

Lyonne Riley published her first book at age five, which was written on tiny sheets of notebook paper, and she insisted on giving a copy to everyone she knew. She's been writing ever since, from fan fiction in her teen years to original fiction as an adult. After a stint in traditional publishing, she discovered what she truly wanted to write: very smutty stories about monsters and the little humans they worship.

Now she lives in the middle of nowhere with her dogs and spouse, writing sexy fairy tales.

Acknowledgments

I would like to thank everyone involved in helping me through the process of putting out this book. I can't say enough how much I appreciate the help and encouragement of the people around me—especially Amber, who told me I could do this in the first place.

Huge thank you to Rowan Woodcock for the gorgeous cover illustration. To my critique partners, who gave me phenomenal feedback: You all make this possible. And of course, my amazing spouse, who has always supported my dreams—and given me lots of inspiration for my characters' sexy adventures.

I couldn't have done this without the expertise of my fellow self-published romance authors. Thank you for inviting me into your circles and helping me through this process.

And thank you to my readers, who gave this book a shot.